THE PRINCE
SHE NEVER KNEW

THE PRINCE
SHE NEVER KNEW

BY

KATE HEWITT

First published in Great Britain 2013
by Mills & Boon, an imprint of Harlequin (UK) Limited,
Large Print edition 2014
Eton House, 18-24 Paradise Road
Richmond, Surrey, TW9 1SR

© 2013 Kate Hewitt

ISBN: 978 0 263 24041 2

Printed and bound in Great Britain
by CPI Antony Rowe, Chippenham, Wiltshire

To Maisey, Caitlin and Jennie,
who first inspired me with the idea for this story!
Love, K.

CHAPTER ONE

TODAY WAS HER wedding day. Alyse Barras gazed at her pale, pinched face in the mirror and decided that not all brides were radiant. As it happened, she looked as if she were on the way to the gallows.

No, she amended, not the gallows; a quick and brutal end was not to be hers, but rather a long, drawn-out life sentence: a loveless marriage to a man whom she barely knew, despite their six-year engagement. Yet even so a small kernel of hope was determined to take root in her heart, to unfurl and grow in the shallowest and poorest of soils.

Maybe he'll learn to love me...

Prince Leo Diomedi of Maldinia seemed unlikely to learn anything of the sort, yet still she hoped. She had to.

'Miss Barras? Are you ready?'

Alyse turned from her reflection to face one of

the wedding coordinator's assistants who stood
in the doorway of the room she'd been given in
the vast royal palace in Averne, Maldinia's capi-
tal city, nestled in the foothills of the Alps.

'As ready as I'll ever be,' she replied, trying to
smile, but everything in her felt fragile, break-
able, and the curve of her lips seemed as if it
could crack her face. Split her apart.

The assistant Marina came forward, looking her
over in the assessing and proprietary way Alyse
had got used to in the three days since she'd arrived in Maldinia—or, really, the six years since
she'd agreed to this engagement. She was a com-
modity to be bought, shaped, presented. An object of great value, to be sure, but still an object.

She'd learned to live with it, although on today
of all days—her wedding day, the day most little
girls dreamed about—she felt the falseness of her
own role more, the sense that her life was simply
something to be staged.

Marina twitched Alyse's veil this way and that,
until she gave a nod of satisfaction. It billowed
gauzily over her shoulders, a gossamer web edged
with three-hundred-year-old lace.

'And now the dress,' Marina said, and flicked

her fingers to indicate that Alyse should turn around.

Alyse moved slowly in a circle as Marina examined the yards of white satin that billowed out behind her, the lace bodice that hugged her breasts and hips and had taken eight top-secret fittings over the last six months. The dress had been the source of intense media speculation, the subject of hundreds of articles in tabloids, gossip magazines, even respected newspapers, television and radio interviews, celebrity and gossip blogs and websites.

What kind of dress would the world's real-life Cinderella—not a very creative way of typecasting her, but it had stuck—wear to marry her very own prince, her one true love?

Well, this. And Alyse had had no say in it at all. It was a beautiful dress, she allowed as she caught a glance of the billowing white satin in the full-length mirror. She could hardly complain. She might have chosen something just like it— if she'd been given a choice.

Marina's walkie-talkie crackled and she spoke into it in rapid Italian, too fast for Alyse to understand, even though she'd been learning Italian ever since she'd become engaged to Leo. It was the native language of his country, and Maldinia's queen-in-waiting should be able to speak it. Unfortunately no one spoke slowly enough for her to be able to understand.

'They're ready.' Marina twitched the dress just as she had the veil and then rummaged on the vanity table for some blusher. 'You look a bit pale,' she explained, and brushed Alyse's cheeks with blusher even though the make-up artist had already spent an hour on her face.

'Thank you,' Alyse murmured. She wished her mother were here, but the royal protocol was—and always had been, according to Queen Sophia—that the bride prepare by herself. Alyse wondered whether that was true. Queen Sophia tended to insist on doing things the way they'd 'always been done' when really it was simply the way she wanted them done. And even though Alyse's mother, Natalie, was Queen Sophia's best friend from their days together at a Swiss boarding school, she clearly didn't want Natalie getting in the way on this most important and august of occasions.

Or so Alyse assumed. She was the bride, and she felt as if she were in the way.

She wondered if she would feel so as a wife.

No. She closed her eyes as Marina next dusted her face with loose powder. She couldn't think like that, couldn't give in to the despair, not on today of all days. She had once before, and it had led only to heartache and regret. Today she wanted to hope, to believe, or at least to try to. Today was meant to be a beginning, not an end.

But if Leo hasn't learned to love me in the last six years, why should he now?

Two months ago, with media interest at a frenzied height, her mother had taken her on a weekend to Monaco. They'd sat in deck chairs and sipped frothy drinks and Alyse had felt herself just begin to relax when Natalie had said, 'You don't have to do this if you don't want to.'

She'd tensed all over again, her drink halfway to her lips. 'Do what?'

'Marry him, Alyse. I know it's all got completely out of hand with the media, and also with the Diomedis, to be frank. But you are still your own woman and I want to make sure you're sure...' Her mother had trailed off, her eyes clouded with anxiety, and Alyse had wondered what she'd guessed.

Did she have even an inkling of how little there was between her and Leo? Few people knew; the world believed they were madly in love, and had done ever since Leo had first kissed her cheek six years ago and the resulting photograph had captured the public's imagination.

Leo's mother Sophia knew, of course, as the pretense of their grand romance had been her idea, Alyse suspected, and of course Leo's father, Alessandro, who had first broached the whole idea to her when she'd been just eighteen years old and starry-eyed over Leo. Perhaps Alexa—Leo's sister, her fiery nature so different from his own sense of cool containment—had guessed.

And, naturally, Leo knew. Leo knew he didn't love her. He just didn't know that for six years she'd been secretly, desperately, loving him.

'I'm happy, Maman,' Alyse had said quietly, and had reached over to squeeze her mother's hand. 'I admit, the media circus isn't my favourite part, but…I love Leo.' She had stumbled only slightly over this unfortunate truth.

'I want for you what your father and I have

had,' Natalie had said, and Alyse had smiled wanly. Her parents' romance was something out of a fairy tale: the American heiress who had captured the heart of a wealthy French financier. Alyse had heard the story many times, how her father had seen her mother across a crowded room—they'd both been attending some important dinner—and he had made his way over to her and said, 'What are you doing with the rest of your life?'

She'd simply smiled and answered, 'Spending it with you.'

Love at first sight. And not just an ordinary, run-of-the-mill love, but of the over-the-top, utterly consuming variety.

Of course her mother wanted that for her. And Alyse would never admit to her how little she actually had, even as she still clung stubbornly to the hope that one day it might become more.

'I'm happy,' she'd repeated, and her mother had looked relieved if not entirely convinced.

Marina's walkie-talkie crackled again, and once again Alyse let the rapid-fire Italian assault her with incomprehension.

'They're waiting,' Marina announced briskly,

and Alyse wondered if she imagined that slightly accusing tone. She'd felt it since she'd arrived in Maldinia, mostly from Queen Sophia: *you're not precisely what we'd have chosen for our son and heir, but you'll have to do. We have no choice, after all.*

The media—the whole world—had made sure of that. There had been no going back from that moment captured by a photographer six years ago when Leo had come to her eighteenth birthday party and brushed his lips against her cheek in a congratulatory kiss. Alyse, instinctively and helplessly, had stood on her tiptoes and clasped her hand to his face.

If she could go back in time, would she change that moment? Would she have turned her face away and stopped all the speculation, the frenzy?

No, she wouldn't have, and the knowledge was galling. At first it had been her love for Leo that had made her agree to their faked fairy tale, but as the years had passed and Leo had shown no interest in loving her—or love at all—she'd considered whether to cut her losses and break off the engagement.

She never had; she'd possessed neither the courage nor conviction to do something that would quite literally have rocked the world. And of course she'd clung to a hope that seemed naïve at best, more likely desperate: that he would learn to love her.

And yet...we get along. We're friends, of a sort. Surely that's a good foundation for marriage?

Always the hope.

'This way, Miss Barras,' Marina said, and ushered her out of the room she'd been getting dressed in and down a long, ornate corridor with marble walls and chandeliers glittering overhead every few feet.

The stiff satin folds of Alyse's dress rustled against the parquet as she followed Marina down the hallway and towards the main entrance of the palace where a dozen liveried footmen stood to attention. She would make the walk to the cathedral across the street and then the far more important walk down the aisle by herself, another Maldinian tradition.

'Wait.' Marina held up a hand and Alyse paused in front of the gilt-panelled doors that led to the front courtyard of the palace where at least a hundred reporters and photographers, probably more, waited to capture this iconic moment. Alyse had had so many iconic moments in the last six years she felt as if her entire adult life had been catalogued in the glossy pages of gossip magazines.

Marina circled her the way Alyse imagined a lion or tiger circled its prey. She was being fanciful, she knew, but her nerves were stretched to breaking point. She'd been in Maldinia for three days and she hadn't seen Leo outside of state functions once. Hadn't spoken to him alone in over a year.

And she was marrying him in approximately three minutes.

Paula, the royal family's press secretary, approached with a brisk click of heels. 'Alyse? You're ready?' she asked in accented English.

She nodded back, not trusting herself to speak.

'Excellent. Now, all you need to remember is to smile. You're Cinderella and this is your glass slipper moment, yes?' She twitched Alyse's veil just as Sophia had done, and Alyse wondered how much more pointless primping she would have to endure. As soon as she stepped outside the veil would probably blow across her face anyway. At least she had enough hair spray in her

7

hair to prevent a single strand from so much as stirring. She felt positively shellacked.

'Cinderella,' she repeated. 'Right.' She'd been acting like Cinderella for six years. She didn't really need the reminder.

'Everyone wants to be you,' Paula continued. 'Every girl, every woman, is dreaming of walking in your shoes right now. And every man wants to be the prince. Don't forget to wave— this is about them as much as you. Include everyone in the fantasy, yes?'

'Right. Yes.' She knew that, had learned it over the years of public attention. And, truthfully, she didn't mind the attention of the crowds, of people who rather incredibly took encouragement and hope from her and her alleged fairy tale of a life. All they wanted from her was friendliness, a smile, a word. All she needed to be was herself.

It was the paparazzi she had trouble with, the constant scrutiny and sense of invasion as rabid journalists and photographers looked for cracks in the fairy-tale image, ways to shatter it completely.

'I'd better get out there before the clock strikes twelve,' she joked, trying to smile, but her mouth was so dry her lips stuck to her teeth. Paula frowned, whipping a tissue from her pocket to blot Alyse's lipstick.

'We're at thirty seconds,' Marina intoned, and Paula positioned Alyse in front of the doors. 'Twenty...'

Alyse knew she was supposed to emerge when the huge, ornate clock on one of the palace's towers chimed the first of its eleven sonorous notes. She would walk sedately, head held high, towards the cathedral as the clock continued chiming and arrive at its doors when the last chime fell into silence.

It had all been choreographed and rehearsed several times, down to the last second. Everything arranged, orchestrated, managed.

'Ten...'

Alyse took a deep breath, or as deep a breath as the tightly fitted bodice of her dress would allow. She felt dizzy, spots dancing before her eyes, although whether from lack of air or sheer nerves she didn't know.

'Five...'

Two footmen opened the doors to the courtyard with a flourish, and Alyse blinked in the sudden brilliance of the sun. The open doorway framed a dazzling blue sky, the two Gothic towers of the cathedral opposite and a huge throng of people.

'Go,' Paula whispered, and gave her a firm nudge in the small of her back.

Pushed by Paula, she moved forward, her dress snagging on her heel so she stumbled ever so slightly. Still it was enough for the paparazzi to notice, and dozens of cameras snapped frantically to capture the moment. Another iconic moment; Alyse could already picture the headlines: *First Stumble on The Road to Happiness?*

She steadied herself, lifted her head and gave the entire viewing world a brilliant smile. The answering cheer roared through the courtyard. Alyse could feel the sound reverberate through her chest, felt her spirits lift at their obvious excitement and approbation.

This was why she was marrying Leo, why the royal family of Maldinia had agreed to his engagement to a mere commoner: because everyone loved her.

Everyone but Leo.

Still smiling, raising one hand in a not-so-regal wave, Alyse started walking towards the cathedral. She heard a few snatched voices amidst the crowd, shouting her name, asking her to turn for a photo. She smiled, leaving the white carpet that had been laid from the palace to the cathedral to shake people's hands, accept posies of flowers.

She was deviating from the remote, regal script she'd been given, but then she always did. She couldn't help but respond to people's warmth and friendliness; all too often it was what strengthened her to maintain this charade that wasn't a charade at all—for her. For Leo, of course, it was.

But maybe, please God, it won't always be...

'Good luck, Alyse,' one starry-eyed teen gushed, clasping her hands tightly. 'You look so beautiful—you really are a princess!'

Alyse squeezed the girl's hands. 'Thank you,' she murmured. 'You look beautiful too, you know. You're glowing more than I am!'

She realised the clock had stopped chiming; she was late. Queen Sophia would be furious, yet it was because of moments like these she was here at all. She didn't stick to the royal family's formalised script; she wrote her own lines without even meaning to and the public loved them.

Except she didn't know what her lines would

be once she was married. She had no idea what she would say to Leo when she finally faced him as his wife.

I love you.

Those were words she was afraid he'd never want to hear.

The cathedral doors loomed in front of her, the interior of the building dim and hushed. Alyse turned one last time towards the crowd and another roar went up, echoing through the ancient streets of Averne. She waved and blew them a kiss, and she heard another cheer. Perhaps the kiss was a bit over the top, but she felt in that moment strangely reckless, almost defiant. There was no going back now.

And then she turned back to the cathedral and her waiting groom.

Leo stood with his back to the doors of the cathedral, but he knew the moment when Alyse had entered. He heard the murmurs fall to an expectant hush, and the roar of approbation that she generated wherever she went had fallen to silence outside. He flexed his shoulders once and remained with his back to the door—and his bride. Maldinian princes did not turn around until the bride had reached the altar and Leo deviated from neither tradition nor duty.

The organ had started playing with sonorous grandeur, some kind of baroque march, and he knew Alyse was walking towards him. He felt a flicker of curiosity; he hadn't seen her dress, had no idea what she looked like in it. Polished, poised and as perfect as usual, he presumed. The perfect bride. The perfect love story. And of course, the perfect marriage. All of it the perfect pretense.

Nothing more.

Finally he felt the folds of her dress whisper against his legs and he turned to face her. He barely noticed the dress. Her face was pale except for two spots of blusher high on her cheekbones. She looked surprisingly nervous, he thought. For the past six years she'd been handling the intense media scrutiny of their engagement with apparent effortless ease, and her attack of nerves now surprised him. Alarmed him a bit too.

She'd agreed to all of this. It was a little late for cold feet.

Conscious of the stares of the congregation—

as well as the cameras televising the ceremony live to millions of people—he smiled and took her hand, which was icy and small in his. He squeezed her fingers, an encouragement if anyone saw, but also a warning. Neither of them could make a mistake now. Too much rode on this marriage, this masquerade. She knew that; so did he. They'd both sold their souls, and willingly.

Now he watched as Alyse lifted her chin, her wide grey eyes flashing with both comprehension and spirit. Her lips curved in a tiny smile and she squeezed his hand back. He felt a flicker of admiration for her courage and poise—as well as one of relief. Crisis averted.

She turned towards the archbishop who was performing the ceremony and he saw the gleam of chestnut hair beneath the lace of her veil, the soft glimmer of a pearl in the shell-like curve of her ear. He turned to face the man as well.

Fifteen minutes later it was done. They'd said their vows and Leo had brushed his lips against Alyse's. He'd kissed her dozens, perhaps hundreds, of times during their engagement, always in front of a crowd. A camera.

He kissed her now as he always had, a firm press of lips that conveyed enthusiasm and even desire without actually feeling either. He didn't want to feel either; he wasn't about to complicate what had been a business arrangement by stirring up a hornet's nest of emotions—either in her or himself.

Although now that they were married, now that they would actually consummate this marriage, he would certainly allow himself to feel attraction at least, a natural desire. All his life he'd controlled such contrary emotions, refused to let them dictate his behaviour as they had his parents'. Refused to let them ruin his life and wreck the monarchy, as they had with his parents.

No, he had more dignity, more self-control, than that. But he certainly intended to take full advantage of his marriage vows—and his marriage bed. It didn't mean his emotions would actually be engaged.

Just his libido.

Leo lifted his head and gazed down at her, smiling slightly for the sake of their audience, and saw that Alyse was gazing at him with panic in her eyes. Her nerves clearly had not abated.

Suppressing his own annoyance, he gently wrapped his hands around hers—they were still icy—and pried them from his shoulders. 'All right?' he murmured.

She nodded, managed a rather sickly smile and turned towards the congregation for their recession down the aisle.

And now it begins, Leo thought. The rest of his life enacting this endless charade, started by a single moment six years ago.

Who could ever have known how a paparazzi photographer would catch that kiss? And not just his lips on her cheek but her hand clasped against his cheek, her face uplifted, eyes shining like silver stars.

That photo had been on the cover of every major publication in the western world. It had been named the third most influential photograph of the century, a fact which made Leo want to bark in cynical laughter. A single, *stupid* kiss influential? Important?

But it had become important, because the sight of the happiness shining from Alyse's eyes had ignited a generation, fired their hearts with faith in love and hope for the future. Some economists credited the photograph with helping to kick-start Europe's economy, a fact Leo thought entirely absurd.

Yet when the monarchy's public relations department had realised the power of that photograph, they had harnessed it for themselves. For him, his father King Alessandro and all the future Diomedis that would reign over Maldinia.

Which had led, inevitably, to this engagement and now marriage, he all the while pretending to live up to what that photograph had promised—because for the public to realise it was nothing more than a fake would be a disaster.

Hand in hand with his bride, he walked down the aisle and into a lifetime of pretending.

She was breaking up, splitting apart, all the fragile, barely held parts of her shattering into pieces. She'd held herself together for so long and now...?

She wasn't sure she could do it any more. And it was too late not to.

Somehow Alyse made it down the aisle, although everything around her—the people, the colours, the noise and light—was a blur. Everything but the look that had flashed in Leo's eyes after he'd kissed her, something bordering on impatient annoyance at her obvious unease. Her panic.

She felt Leo's arm like a band of iron beneath her hand. 'Smile as we come out of the cathedral,' he murmured, and then the crowds were upon them, their roar loud in their ears and, still feeling sick inside, she smiled for all she was worth.

The wordless roar turned into a rhythmic chant: *bacialo! Bacialo!*

The crowd wanted them to kiss. Wordlessly, Alyse turned to Leo, tilted her head up at him as he gazed down at her and stroked her cheek with a single fingertip and then, once again, brushed his lips against her in another emotionless kiss.

Even so that cool kiss touched Alyse's soul, whispered its impossible hopes into her heart. She kept her lips mostly slack beneath his, knowing after six years of such kisses he didn't want her to respond, never had. No hot, open-mouthed kisses of passion for them. Just these chaste displays of their mutual love and devotion.

He lifted his head and she smiled and waved to the crowd. It was done.

Still smiling, Leo led her to the waiting carriage, all gilt and scrollwork, like something out of a fairy tale. A Cinderella carriage for a Cinderella bride.

He helped her in and then sat next to her on the narrow leather seat, his thigh pressing against her hip, her dress billowing over his lap. The liveried coachman closed the door and they were off for a celebratory ride through the city, then back to the palace for the reception.

As soon as the door had closed, Leo's smile, his mask, dropped. There was no need for it now; no one was watching. He turned to her, a frown appearing between his brows.

'You're too pale.'

'I'm sorry,' she murmured. 'I'm tired.'

Leo's frown deepened, and then it ironed out and he sighed and raked his hands through his hair. 'It's no wonder. The last few days have been exhausting. I expect it will be good to get away.'

They were leaving tomorrow for a ten-day honeymoon: first a week on a private Caribbean island and then a whistle-stop tour through London, Paris and Rome.

Alyse's insides quaked as she thought of that first week. An entire week alone, without cameras or crowds, no one to perform for, no audience to entertain. A week completely by themselves.

She lived in both hope and fear of that week.

'Yes,' she said now, and thankfully her voice remained steady, strong. 'I expect it will.'

Leo turned to the window and waved at the crowds lining the ancient cobbled streets of Averne, and Alyse turned to her own window and waved as well. Each flutter of her fingers drained her, as if she were lifting a huge weight. Her engagement ring, an enormous emerald surrounded by pearls and diamonds, sparkled in the sun.

She didn't know why everything felt so much harder now. She'd been living this life for six years, after all. She'd come to enjoy her interactions with the public and had learned to live with the media's attention.

Yet today, on her wedding day, with nearly the last words she'd spoken having been vows before the world, before *God*…

She felt the falseness of their masquerade more than ever. They'd only been married a few minutes and already she felt how difficult, how draining, this life of play-acting was going to be. She'd been moving towards that realisation for months as the weight had dropped off and her stomach had churned with nerves, as everything had steamrolled ahead with such frightening implacability that she had known she couldn't call a halt to the proceedings even if she'd wanted to. The pretending.

And the terrible truth was, she *still* didn't want to. She'd still rather hope.

'Alyse?'

She turned from the window where she'd been blindly staring at the crowds, her hand rising and falling in a fluttering wave without even realising she was doing so. 'Yes?'

'You don't look well,' Leo said and he sounded concerned. 'Do you need a few moments to rest before we go into the reception?'

Alyse knew what the reception would entail: hours of chatting, laughing and pretending to be in love. Of kissing Leo, squeezing his hand and laying her head on his shoulder. She'd done it all before, of course, but now it hurt more. It felt, absurdly perhaps, more fake.

'I'm fine.' She smiled and turned back to the window so he wouldn't see how her smile trembled and almost slid right off her face. 'I'm fine,' she said again, this time for herself, because she needed to believe it. She was stronger than this. She had to be stronger, because she'd chosen this life, knowing how hard it would be.

At times it might have felt as if she had no choice, with the pressure of both the media and the monarchy urging her to agree, but if she'd really wanted to break off the engagement she surely could have. She would have found the strength to.

No, she'd chosen this life, and chosen Leo; she'd believed in the duty she was performing and she'd held out for love.

She still did. Today was a beginning, she reminded herself. Today was the start of her and Leo's life together, days and nights spent with each other in a way neither of them had ever experienced before. Maybe, finally, Leo would fall in love with her.

Leo just wanted this day to be over. Although of course with its end would come a whole new, and rather interesting, complication: the night. Their wedding night.

He glanced again at Alyse; her face was turned

away from him but he could still see how pale
and wan she looked. And thin. The dress clung
to her figure, which had already been slender but
now looked rather waif-like. Clearly the strain
of the heightened media attention had got to her
over these last few months.

Just as it had got to him. He'd lived his life in
the spotlight and he certainly should be used to
it now. As a child, the play-acting for the media
had confused him, but as he'd grown older he'd
accepted it as the price he had to pay for the sake
of his duty to the crown. At least this time, with
Alyse, he'd chosen it. He'd entered this loveless
marriage willingly, even happily.

Because wasn't it better to know love was a
sham from the beginning, than to live in desperate yearning for it—just as he had done for the
whole of his confused and unhappy childhood?

At least he and Alyse agreed on that. She'd always known he didn't love her, and he knew she
didn't love him. Really, it was the perfect foundation for a marriage: agreed and emotionless
expectations.

Yet he'd found the last few months of intense
media speculation and interest wearying. The

charade of acting as if they were in love had started to wear thin. And he'd wondered, not for the first time, just why Alyse had agreed to this marriage.

He'd never asked her, had never wanted to know. It was enough that she'd agreed, and she'd gone along with it ever since. Just as he had.

Only, unlike him, she had no incentive to please the press, no duty to repair a badly damaged monarchy and increase the tourist revenue for a small and struggling country. No need to pretend to be wildly in love. So why had she agreed all those years ago? Why had she continued to agree?

He had to assume it was because, like him, she wanted this kind of marriage. Or maybe she just wanted this kind of life—the life of a princess and one day a queen. He didn't fault her for it. She wouldn't be the first person to have her head turned by wealth and fame. In any case, she'd approached their union with a practical acceptance he admired, and she'd embraced the public as much as they'd embraced her.

Really, she was perfect. So why did he wonder? Why did he now feel a new, creeping uncertainty?

The questions—and the lack of answers—annoyed him. He liked certainty and precision; he prided himself on both.

He didn't want to wonder about his bride on his wedding day. Didn't want to worry about why she looked so pale and shaky, or why her smile seemed less assured. He wanted things to be simple, straightforward, as they had been for the last six years.

There was no reason for marriage to complicate matters, he told himself.

The carriage came to a stop in front of the palace and he turned to her with a faint smile, determined to banish his brooding thoughts and keep their relationship on the courteous yet impersonal footing they'd maintained for their entire engagement.

'Shall we?' he said, one eyebrow lifted, and Alyse managed just as faint a smile back as she took his hand and allowed him to help her out of the carriage.

CHAPTER TWO

THEY WERE ALONE. Every muscle in Alyse's body ached with exhaustion, yet even so she could not keep a heart-stopping awareness of Leo from streaking through her as he closed the door behind them.

They'd retired to the tower suite, a sumptuous bedroom, bathroom and dressing-room all housed in one of the stone turrets of the ancient royal palace. A fire blazed in the hearth and a huge four-poster bed with silk coverings and sheets took up the main part of the room. Alyse stared at the white silk and lace negligee laid out on the bed and swallowed hard.

She and Leo had never talked about *this*.

They should have, she supposed, but then they had never really talked about anything. Their relationship—and she could only use that word loosely—had been little more than a long-term publicity stunt. Conversation had been limited to managing their appearances together.

And now they were married. It felt, at least to her, like a complete game-changer. Until now they'd only experienced manufactured moments lived in the public eye; but here, for the first time, they were alone with no need for pretence.

Would *this* moment be real?

'Relax,' Leo said, coming up behind her. Alyse felt his breath on the back of her neck and she suppressed a shiver of both anticipation and nervousness. 'We've been waiting for six years; we don't need to rush things.'

'Right,' she murmured, and then he moved past her to the window. The latticed shutters were thrown open to a starlit sky. Earlier in the evening there had been fireworks all over the city; the celebrations of their marriage had gone on all day.

It was only now that the city's joy was finally subsiding, everyone heading back to his or her home—and Alyse and Leo to this honeymoon suite.

She watched as Leo loosened his black tie. He'd changed into a tuxedo for the evening party, and she into a designer gown chosen by the team of stylists hired to work on her. It was pale pink, strapless, with a frothy skirt. A Cinderella dress.

'Do you want to change?' Leo asked as he undid the top few studs of his shirt. Standing there, framed by the window, the ends of his bow-tie dangling against the crisp whiteness of his shirt, he looked unbearably handsome. His hair was a glossy midnight-black, and rumpled from where he'd carelessly driven his fingers through it.

His eyes were dark too—once Alyse had thought they were black but she'd learned long ago from having had to gaze adoringly up into them so many times they were actually a very dark blue.

And his body... She might not have seen it in all of its bare glory, but he certainly wore a suit well. Broad shoulders, trim hips, long and powerful legs, every part of him declared he was wonderfully, potently male.

Would she see that body tonight? Would she caress and kiss it, give in to the passion she knew she could feel for him if he let her?

And what about him? Would he feel it?

In the course of six years, he'd always been solicitous, considerate, unfailingly polite. She couldn't fault him, and yet she'd yearned for more. For emotion, passion and, yes, always love. She'd always been drawn to the intensity she felt pulsing latent beneath his coolness, the passion she wanted to believe could be unleashed if he ever freed himself from the bonds of duty and decorum. If he ever revealed himself to her.

Would he tonight, if just a little? Or would this part of their marriage be a masquerade as well?

'I suppose I'll change,' she said, her gaze sliding inexorably to the negligee laid out for both their perusals.

'You don't need to wear that,' Leo said, and he let out an abrupt laugh, the sound without humour. 'There's no point, really, is there?'

Wasn't there? Alyse felt a needle of hurt burrow under her skin, into her soul. What did he want her to wear, if not that?

'Why don't you take a bath?' he suggested. 'Relax. It's been a very long day.' He turned away from her, yanking off his tie, and after a moment Alyse headed to the bathroom, telling herself she was grateful for the temporary reprieve. They could both, perhaps, use a little time apart.

We've basically had six years apart.

Swallowing hard, she turned on the taps.

There were no clothes in the bathroom, something she should have realised before she got in the tub. Two sumptuous terry-cloth robes hung on the door, and after soaking in the bath for a good half-hour Alyse slipped one on, the sleeves coming past her hands and the hem nearly skimming her ankles. She tied it securely, wondering what on earth would happen now. What she wanted to happen.

For Leo to gasp at the sight of me and sweep me into his arms, admit the feelings he's been hiding all along...

Fantasies, pathetic fantasies, and she *knew* that. She wasn't expecting a lightning bolt of love to strike Leo; she just wanted to start building something, something real. And that took time.

Tonight was a *beginning*.

Taking a deep breath, stealing herself for whatever lay ahead, she opened the door.

Leo had changed out of his tuxedo and now wore a pair of navy-blue silk draw-string pyjama bottoms and nothing else. He sat sprawled in a chair by the fire, a tumbler of whisky cradled in his hands, the amber liquid glinting in the firelight.

Alyse barely noticed any of that; her gaze was ensnared by the sight of his bare chest. She'd never seen it before, not in the flesh, although there had been several paparazzi photographs of him in swimming trunks while on holiday—though not with her. They'd never actually had a holiday together in six years' engagement.

Seeing his chest now, up close and in the glorious flesh, was another thing entirely. His skin was bronzed, the fire casting long shadows on the taut flesh and sculpted muscle. She could see dark whorls of hair on his chest, veeing down to the loose waistband of his trousers slung low on his lean hips, and her heart felt as if it had flipped right over in her chest. He was just so beautiful.

He glanced up as she approached, and his lips twitched in sardonic amusement as he took in her huge robe. 'I think that one's mine.'

'Oh.' She blushed, and then as she imagined Leo attempting to wear the smaller, woman's-sized robe, a sudden bubble of nervous laughter escaped her. He arched an eyebrow and she came forward to explain. 'I was picturing you in the other robe. Mine, apparently.'

'An interesting image.' His lips twitched again in a tiny smile and her heart lightened ridiculously. All she needed was a smile. A single smile on which to build a world of dreams.

She sat in the chair opposite his and stretched her bare feet towards the fire. Neither of them spoke for several minutes, the only sound the comforting crackle and spit of the flames.

'This is strange,' Alyse finally said softly, her gaze still on the fire. She heard Leo shift in his seat.

'It's bound to be, I suppose.'

She glanced upwards and saw his face was half in darkness, the firelight casting flickering shadows over the other half. She could see the hard plane of one cheek, the dark glint of stubble on his jaw, the pouty fullness of his sculpted lips. He had the lips of a screen siren, yet he was unabashedly, arrogantly male.

She'd felt those lips on her own so many times, cool brushes of mouths when what she wanted, what she *craved*, was hot, mindless passion—

tongues tangling, plunging, hands moving and groping...

She forced the images, and the resulting heat, away from her mind and body.

'Do you realise,' she said, trying to keep her tone light, and even teasing, although they'd never actually teased each other, 'we haven't actually been alone together in about a year?'

He shrugged one bare, powerful shoulder. 'That's not all that surprising, considering.'

She glanced back at the fire, tucking her now-warmed feet underneath the hem of her robe. 'Considering what?'

'Considering we've been living separate lives ever since we announced this sham of an engagement.'

Alyse swallowed. 'I know that.' Neither of them had been in a rush to get married. Leo certainly hadn't, and Alyse had already accepted a place at Durham University. Her parents hadn't wanted her to give it up for marriage at eighteen, and neither had she, although she suspected Queen Sophia could have bullied her into it.

She'd been so young then, so naïve and overwhelmed. She liked to think she'd changed, that she'd grown up, at least a bit. She hoped she had, but right now she felt as gauche as ever.

At any rate, a long engagement had fed the media frenzy, accomplishing the monarchy's purposes of keeping them in positive press for over half a decade. For the last six years she'd been living in England, completing her BA and then her MA in European history—a subject the monarchy had considered acceptable for its future queen, since it could be relevant to her rule. Alyse just loved history.

She'd wanted to have some kind of normalcy in her life, some kind of separation from Leo and the feelings he stirred up in her; from the bizarre intensity of life in the media spotlight and under the monarchy's critical eye.

University had thankfully given her a degree of that normalcy she'd craved. Out of respect, and perhaps even love for her, the paparazzi hadn't followed her too closely.

She'd had a somewhat usual university experience—or as usual as it could be, considering the jaunts to royal functions every few weeks, her carefully choreographed appearances with Leo and the constant curiosity and speculation of the other students and even some of the tutors and lecturers.

Remembering it all now brought a sudden lump to her throat. No matter how normal her life had seemed on the surface, she'd still felt the loneliness of being different from the other students. Of knowing the paltry truth of her relationship with Leo.

It was a knowledge that had sometimes led to despair, and that had once led to a foolish choice and a heartache and shame that even now could bring her to a cringing blush.

She pushed the memory away. It had no place here and now, on her wedding night.

'But we're not going to live separate lives now,' she said and Leo inclined his head in brief acknowledgement.

'I suppose we need to decide how we want to conduct our marriage, now that we'll be under the same roof.' He paused to take a long swallow of whisky, and Alyse watched the movement of the corded muscles of his throat, felt a spasm of helpless longing. 'I don't see any real reason to change things too much,' he continued. Her longing left her in a rush.

She felt the way you did when you thought there was one more step in a staircase, the jolt going right through her bones to her soul. Had she actually thought things would change that much now they were married? That Leo would? It would mean more pretending, not less. Yet how could they pretend *that* much?

'Things will have to change a bit, I imagine,' she said, trying to speak lightly. 'I mean…we're married. It's different.'

'Assuredly, but it doesn't mean we have to be different, does it?' He glanced at her, eyebrows raised, cool smile in place. 'The last six years have worked out quite well, don't you think?'

No. *No, no, no.* Yet how could she disagree with him when she'd been acting like she'd agreed with him all along? Alyse swallowed. 'I suppose, but now we have a chance to actually get to know each other…' She trailed off uncertainly, wanting him to leap in and agree. When would she learn? He wasn't going to do that. He wasn't that kind of man.

Leo frowned, then turned back to the fire. 'We've always had that chance,' he answered after a moment. 'We just chose not to take it.'

'I suppose,' Alyse managed. She tried not to let his words hurt her; he didn't mean to be cruel; he simply had no idea of how she felt, never had. This wasn't his fault, it was hers, for agreeing to pretend for so long. For never having been honest with him about how she really felt.

'It might get a bit tedious,' she ventured. 'Pretending for so long. We'll have to appear together more often, I mean.'

'Oh, the media will get tired of us eventually,' Leo said dismissively. He gave her a quick, cool smile, his eyes hard and glinting. 'Especially once the next generation comes along.'

The next generation. Their children. Alyse felt her heart start to thud.

He put his glass down, raking both hands through his hair so Alyse's gaze was drawn to the ripple of muscles in his arms and chest, the sculpted beauty of his body. Desire twisted and writhed inside her like some desperate, untamed creature seeking its freedom.

Leo dropped his hands and gave her a measured look. 'I know tonight is bound to be awkward, at least at first.' He nodded towards the huge bed looming behind them. 'I think if we acknowledge that up front, it might be easier.'

Alyse's mouth felt like sandpaper as she stared at him. 'Yes, probably it will be.' She tried for a light tone, or at least as matter-of-fact as his. She wasn't sure she managed either. 'Much better to be upfront and honest with each other from the start.' She forced a smile, knowing her words for lies. 'We pretend enough as it is.'

'Exactly.' Leo nodded in approval. 'It's one thing to pretend to the press, but I hope we can always be honest with each other.'

She nodded back mechanically. 'That…would be good.'

'Don't look so terrified,' Leo said dryly. He nodded once more towards the bed. 'I hope we can find a little pleasure there at least.'

A little pleasure? His words stung. 'I'm not terrified,' she told him crisply. 'It's just— It's a bit awkward, like you said; that's all.'

'Naturally. I'll do my best to alleviate that awkwardness, of course.'

She heard a thread of amusement in his voice, saw it in his cool smile, and knew that being made love to by Leo wouldn't be awkward at all. It would be wonderful.

Except it wouldn't be making love. It would be cold, emotionless sex. A physical act, a soulless transaction. 'A little pleasure', indeed. She closed her eyes, hating the thought. Hating the fact that she had to pretend, would always have to pretend, not just with the press but with him. It would be so, so much harder now. Why hadn't she realised that?

'Alyse,' Leo said, and she opened her eyes. He was leaning forward, his eyes narrowed in concern. 'If you'd rather, we can wait. We don't have to consummate our marriage tonight.'

'A reprieve?' she said, her voice sounding cynical even to her own ears.

'It might be more pleasant when we're not so tired and there are fewer expectations on us,' Leo answered with a shrug. 'And frankly, no matter what you've said, you do look terrified.'

Yes, she was, but not in the way he thought. She wasn't afraid of sex. She was afraid of it being meaningless for Leo. Did he want her at all? Was this a bore for him, a *chore*?

'I promise you, I'm not afraid,' she said when

she trusted herself to speak as neutrally as he had. 'But I am tired, so perhaps this…aspect of our marriage can wait a little while.'

Leo shrugged, as if he didn't care either way, and that hurt too. 'Of course. But we should both sleep in the bed. Staff see everything, and even palace employees have been known to gossip.'

She nodded, trying not to imagine lying next to Leo, his nearly bare body so close to hers. It was a big bed, after all. And she needed to learn how to manage this kind of situation. They would, after all, be sleeping in the same bed for the next…

Except, no; perhaps they wouldn't. Perhaps they would have separate bedrooms along with separate lives, coming together only for the cameras or to create an heir.

'That's fine,' she said. 'I'll just put some…' She trailed off, because the only clothes in the room were her ballgown and the negligee. She didn't like either option.

Leo glanced at the lace confection spread out on the bed. 'It's a big bed,' he said dryly. 'And I think I can control myself, even if you wear that bit of nonsense.'

Alyse swallowed, nodded. Even tried to smile, though every careless word he spoke felt like a dagger thrust to her heart. She didn't want him to be able to control himself. She'd always known him to be cool, pragmatic, even ruthless. Yet she wanted him to be different with her, and she was honest enough to recognise that some stupid, schoolgirl part of her had secretly hoped things might change when they were finally alone.

'Fine,' she said and, rising from the chair, she went to the bed and swept the negligee from it before disappearing into the bathroom once more.

Leo stretched out on one side of the bed and waited for Alyse to emerge from the bathroom. He felt the conversation hadn't gone as well as he would have liked. Alyse had seemed brittle, almost as if he'd hurt her feelings, a possibility which exasperated him. He'd thought she was as pragmatic as he was about their union, yet this new, unexpected awkwardness clearly unnerved her—as well as him.

When had he started caring about her feelings, whether she felt nervous, awkward or afraid? The whole point of this marriage, this pretence, was that he didn't have to care. He didn't have to engage emotions he'd purposely kept dormant for so long.

And while he might be weary of pretending—he'd done enough of it in his life, God only knew—at least this marriage, this pretence, had been his choice. His decision.

He still remembered the negotiation they'd gone through after that wretched photograph had gone viral. His father had asked to see them privately.

Alyse had flown to Maldinia a few weeks after her birthday party; her mother had accompanied her. And, when she'd walked into his father's private study alone, Leo had been jolted by how young and vulnerable she looked, dressed simply in a plain skirt and schoolgirl's blouse, her dark hair held back in a ponytail.

His father hadn't minced words; he never did. Queen Sophia and her mother were friends, he told Alyse, and they'd considered a match between her and Leo. Leo knew that hadn't exactly been true; his mother had wanted someone with slightly bluer blood than Alyse's to marry her son. Leo had gone to that birthday party with only a vague and passing knowledge of Alyse's existence and it was the media hype that had turned it into something else entirely.

'In an ideal world,' King Alessandro had said with a geniality Leo knew his father did not remotely possess, *'you would have got to know each other, courted. Seen if you suited. But it's not an ideal world.'*

Alyse had simply stared.

Leo, of course, had known where this was going all along. He'd talked to his parents already, had received the assignment from on high. *You must marry her, Leo. The public adores her. Think of what it will do for your country, your kingship.*

He'd known what they really meant: what it would do for them. They'd done enough damage to Maldinia's monarchy with their lies, affairs and careless spending. He was the only one left to clean up the mess.

He'd understood all that, but Alyse hadn't. She'd just looked thunderstruck. She'd barely spoken for that whole meeting, just listened as the King went on about the benefits of a 'decided' marriage—a much more innocuous term than *arranged,* Leo had thought cynically. Or *commanded.*

She'd only spoken when she'd begun to perceive, dimly, just what kind of charade they would be perpetuating and for how long. 'You mean,' she'd said in a voice only a little above a whisper, 'we have to…to *pretend* we're in love?'

'Feelings come in time, don't they?' Alessandro had answered with that same false joviality, and Leo had looked away. *No, they didn't.* If Alessandro held up his own marriage, his own family, as an example, it showed they never came. And you couldn't trust them anyway.

But Alyse had nodded slowly, accepting, and their engagement had been announced the next day along with them posing for requisite photos.

And the rest, Leo thought now, lacing his arms above his head, was history. Repeating itself over and over again.

The door to the bathroom opened and Alyse emerged, wearing the woman's robe. Leo wondered if she'd try to sleep in that bulky thing. He supposed a little virginal shyness was natural.

He watched as she skirted the bed and then hesitated on the far side, her fingers playing with the sash of her robe. Leo reached for his bed-side lamp.

'Shall I turn out the light?'

'If you like.'

Actually, he didn't like. He was suddenly rather curious as to what Alyse looked like in the skimpy negligee. He'd seen her in plenty of designer dresses and well-coordinated outfits, hair and make-up immaculately styled, always primped to perfection.

But he'd never seen her like this—wearing a bridal nightgown, her chestnut hair loose about her shoulders, grey eyes wide, about to climb into his bed. He felt an insistent stirring of arousal; it had been a long time since he'd been with a woman. A *very* long time.

He switched the light off, but the moon spilling through the open windows was enough to see by anyway, and as he lay back against the pillows he saw her slip the bulky robe from her body. Dressed as she was in only the slinky negligee, the moon gilded her slender curves in silver.

He could see the shadowy vee between her breasts, the dip of her waist, the hidden juncture of her thighs. Then she slid hurriedly under the covers and lay there, rigid and unmoving.

Leo had never felt so far from sleep and, judging by how she lay there like a board, he suspected Alyse was the same. Perhaps they should have agreed to consummate their marriage tonight. At least it would have given them something to do.

He considered talking to her, but after six years of enacting this parody of love he had nothing of consequence to say, and he didn't think she had either. Which was how he'd wanted it.

Yet in the darkness and silence of that moment he felt a sudden, surprising need for conversation, even connection. Something he'd taught himself never to crave.

And he had no idea how to go about creating it now.

'Goodnight,' he finally said, his voice coming out gruffer than he'd meant it to, and he felt Alyse tense even more next to him.

'Goodnight,' she answered back, her voice so soft and sad that Leo felt caught between re-

morse and exasperation at her obvious emotion—
and his.

With a barely suppressed sigh, he rolled onto
his side, his back to Alyse, and willed himself
to sleep.

CHAPTER THREE

ALYSE AWOKE GRITTY-EYED and still feeling exhausted. Lying next to Leo, she hadn't slept well, conscious of his hard, powerful form just inches away from her even when she'd been falling into a restless doze.

Now as sunlight streamed through the windows she wondered what the day would bring. They were meant to fly to St Cristos, a private island in the Caribbean, that morning to begin their honeymoon. A week completely alone, without the distractions of television, telephones, computers or any other people at all. A week, she still hoped, when they could get to know one another properly, or even at all.

A knock sounded at the door and before Alyse could say or even think anything Leo was snaking his arm around her waist, drawing her close against the seductive heat of his body. Shock turned her rigid as she felt the hard contours

of his chest and thigh against her backside—
and then the unmistakable press of his erection
against her bottom.

'*Vieni,*' he called and then murmured against
her hair, 'Sorry, but the staff will gossip.'

Alyse barely took in his words. She'd never
been so close to him, every part of her body in
exquisite contact with his. The crisp hair on his
chest tickled her bare shoulders, and the feel of
his arousal pressing insistently against her bottom sent sizzling darts of sensation shooting
through her.

She shifted instinctively, although whether she
was drawing away or closer to him she didn't
even know. She felt a new, dizzying need spiral
up inside her as his own hips flexed instinctively
back. Leo groaned under his breath and his arm
came even more firmly around her. 'Stop wrig-
gling,' he whispered, 'Or I might embarrass myself. I'm only human, you know.'

It took a few seconds for his meaning to pen-
etrate the fog of her dazed mind, and by that
time two young serving women were wheeling
in a breakfast tray, the smell of fresh coffee and
breakfast rolls on the air.

Embarrass himself? Was he actually implying that he wanted her that much? That a mere wriggle of hips could send him over the edge?

Leo let go of her, straightening in bed as he adjusted the duvet over himself. *'Grazie,'* he said and the two women giggled and blushed as they left the room, casting covert looks at the two of them in bed. Alyse realised the strap of her negligee had fallen off one shoulder, and her hair was a tangled mass about her face. Did she look like a woman who had been pleasured and loved? She felt like a mess.

She tucked her tangled hair behind her ears and willed her heart rate to slow. Despite the obvious evidence of his arousal, Leo now looked completely unfazed and indifferent as he slid out of bed and went to the breakfast tray to pour them both coffee.

'Sorry about that. Basic bodily function, at least for a man in the morning. I think we convinced the staff, at any rate.'

Disappointment crashed through her. *Basic bodily function.* So, no, it had had nothing to do with her in particular. Of course it didn't. 'It's fine,' Alyse murmured. She took a steadying breath and forced herself to meet his wry gaze. 'We're married, after all.'

'So we are.' He handed her a cup of coffee and sipped his own, his expression turning preoccupied over the rim of the porcelain cup. 'But I imagine all this pretending will get tiresome for both of us after a while.'

Alyse stared into the fragrant depths of her coffee. 'Like you said, the press will get bored of us now that we're married. As long as we seem happy in public, they won't really care.' It hurt to say it, to imply that that was what she wanted.

'Perhaps.' Leo nodded slowly, and Alyse imagined he was wondering just how soon he could return to his simple, solitary life.

And when he did what would she do? Over the last few months she'd bolstered her flagging spirits by reminding herself that, just like Leo, she had a duty. A role. As princess and later Queen of Maldinia she would encourage and love her people. She would involve herself in her country, its charities and industry, and in doing so bring hope to a nation.

She tried to hold onto that idea now, but it seemed like so much airy, arrogant nonsense when she considered how the majority of her days were likely to be spent: in loneliness and isolation, separated from a husband who was perfectly happy with their business arrangement.

'When do we leave for St Cristos?' she asked, not wanting either of them to dwell on the bleak future they both clearly envisioned.

'We leave the palace at eleven o'clock for a public appearance in the front courtyard. Photo opportunity and all that.' He smiled and Alyse saw the cynicism in the twist of his lips, the flatness in his navy eyes. He never used to be so cynical, she thought. Pragmatic, yes, and even cold, but he'd approached their engagement with a brisk and accepting efficiency she'd tried to match, rather than this jaded resentment.

Was he feeling as she did, that marriage had changed something between them, made it worse? Pretending *after* the vows had been said seemed a greater travesty than before, something she'd never considered as Leo's fiancée. She didn't think Leo had considered it either.

'I'll leave you to get dressed,' he said, putting down his coffee cup. 'I'll meet you downstairs in the foyer a few minutes before eleven.'

Wordlessly Alyse nodded, seeing the practicality of it yet feeling a needling disappointment anyway. Was every interaction going to involve a way to avoid each other? Would her life consist of endless awkward exchanges without any real intimacy or emotion, *ever*? Something would have to change. She couldn't live like this; she wouldn't.

Maybe, she thought with no more than a flicker of weary hope, it would change on St Cristos.

Several hours later they boarded the royal jet and Leo disappeared into a study in the rear of the plane. Alyse had been on the jet before when she'd flown between England and Maldinia, yet the opulent luxury always amazed her. Her own family was wealthy and privileged—her father had built a financial empire and her mother had been an heiress—but they weren't this kind of rich. They weren't royal.

You are now.

It still felt unreal. If she didn't actually feel like Leo's wife, how would she ever feel like a princess? Like a queen?

Pushing the thought aside, she made herself comfortable on one of the leather sofas in the main cabin of the plane. Just as planned, she and Leo had made their appearance outside the palace doors. A crowd had surrounded the palace; posies and bouquets of flowers had been piled up by the gates. Alyse had spent a few minutes chatting, smiling and laughing, while Leo had looked on, his smile faint and a little bit wooden. While the people loved the handsome, enigmatic prince, he didn't engage the crowds the way she did, and never had. This, she knew, was why Maldinia's monarchy needed her. Why Leo needed her.

Nothing else.

Now, with the crowds and reporters gone, she wondered just how she and Leo would spend their time alone. Judging by the way he'd disappeared into the jet's study, *alone* was the operative word.

She felt a sudden stab of annoyance, which at least felt stronger than the misery that had been swamping her since their marriage. No matter how fake their relationship was, Leo's determined ignoring of her was just plain rude.

Fuelled by her outrage, Alyse rose from the sofa and went to find Leo in the study. He sat at a desk, his dark head bent over a sheaf of papers. He was dressed for travel in a crisp blue button-down shirt and dark trousers, but he still looked magnificent, his muscles taut and powerful underneath the starched cotton of his shirt. He glanced up as she approached, his dark brows snapping together.

'What is it?'

'I just wondered if you intended to spend the entire time in your study,' she said, her voice coming out close to a snap, and Leo looked at her in something close to bewilderment.

'Does it matter?'

Impatience warred with hurt. 'A bit, Leo. I understand you don't want things to change between us, but a little conversation could be nice. Or are we going to spend the next week trying to avoid each other?'

He still looked flummoxed, and now also a bit annoyed. 'I'm not trying to avoid you.'

'It just comes naturally, then?'

'We've been on this plane for ten minutes,' he replied, his voice becoming so very even. 'Don't you think you can entertain yourself for a little while longer?'

Alyse shook her head impatiently. She could

see how Leo might think she was being unreasonable, but it was so much more than this one journey. 'I can entertain myself just fine,' she said. 'But I don't particularly enjoy living in isolation.'

Leo's mouth thinned into a hard line. 'The plane will take off in a few minutes. I'll join you in the cabin before it does.'

His words seemed so grudgingly given, yet Alyse knew at this point it was better simply to accept them at face value. Now was not the time to force a confrontation, to confess that she didn't think she could live like this for so much as a morning, much less a lifetime. This was, after all, what she'd agreed to all those years ago when King Alessandro had spelled it out so plainly.

Feelings come in time, don't they? She'd built her hopes on that one throwaway remark, clearly meant only to appease her. She'd lived for six years believing it could be true. She might as well have built castles in the air.

Leo had already turned back to his papers, so after a second's uneasy pause Alyse turned around and went to the cabin.

He didn't come out for take-off. Her annoyance

turned to a simmering anger as the staff served her sparkling water instead of the champagne left chilling in a bucket, clearly meant for the two of them to toast their marriage.

She avoided their eyes and reached for her e-reader, bitterly glad she'd filled it with newly purchased books before she'd left. Clearly she'd be getting a lot of reading done on her honeymoon.

A few hours into the flight Leo finally made an appearance. 'Sorry about that,' he said, sitting across from her. 'I had a bit of work to catch up on before we go off the grid.'

Despite his casually made apology, Alyse couldn't let go of her anger. 'If you don't want your staff to gossip, perhaps you should be a bit more attentive to your bride,' she answered tartly. 'We've only been married for one day, you know.'

Leo stared at her, nonplussed. 'Even couples wildly in love have work to do.'

'Even on their honeymoon?'

He narrowed his gaze. 'I have a duty to my country—'

'This whole marriage is about duty.' She cut him off and realised too late how shrewish and hurt she sounded. How ridiculous, considering the nature of their relationship.

'Careful,' he said softly, glancing at the closed cabin doors.

'Our whole life is going to be about being careful,' she retorted before she could stop herself. She hated how her hurt was spilling out of her. She'd kept it hidden for so long, why was she weakening now?

'And you always knew that.' The glance he gave her was repressive. 'I think we should save this conversation for another, more private time.'

'At least I have a conversation to look forward to, then.' Leo just stared at her, and Alyse looked away, trying to reclaim some of the cool composure she'd cloaked herself with during the last few years. She'd never lit into him like this, never showed him how much his indifference hurt her or how much more she wanted from him.

'What's wrong with you?' he asked after a moment and he sounded both curious and exasperated. 'You've never acted like this before.'

'We've never been alone like this before,' she answered, her face still averted. 'I just don't want you to ignore or avoid me for the entire week. I'll go crazy.'

Leo was silent for a long moment. 'I don't mean to ignore or avoid you,' he said finally. 'I'm just acting as we always have. I thought you accepted the nature of our relationship—preferred it, as I do.'

Alyse struggled to keep her face composed, her voice even, but his words hurt so much. Too much. 'I've accepted it,' she said carefully. 'But it feels different now. We're married, after all, and we're going to spend more time together. Time alone. It would be nice if we could enjoy it, at least.'

That was so much less than she wanted, but at least it was a start—if Leo agreed.

He didn't answer, just reached for the champagne and poured two flutes, the bubbles fizzing and bursting against the crystal sides. 'I suppose that's not an unreasonable request,' he said eventually, and Alyse didn't know whether to laugh or cry at his grudging tone.

'I'm glad you think so,' she answered, and accepted a glass of champagne.

He eyed her evenly. 'I suppose we should have

discussed our expectations of what our married life would look like beforehand.'

'Would it have made any difference?'

'Not to me, perhaps.' He raised his glass. 'To what shall we toast?'

Alyse couldn't think of a single thing. 'To the future,' she finally said, and heard the bleakness in her voice. 'Whatever it may hold.'

Nodding in acceptance, Leo drank.

Leo watched Alyse slowly raise the flute of champagne to her lips. Her face was pale, her eyes wide and dark. She looked rather unbearably sad, he thought, and he had no idea why. What did she want from him? And why, after so long accepting the status quo, did she seem to want things to change?

Shifting in his seat, he turned towards the window. Outside the sky was an endless, brilliant blue. He thought of the week they were to spend on St Cristos, which was apparently the most elite honeymoon destination in the world—chosen, of course, to perpetuate the myth of their relationship. The relationship—a word he didn't even like to use—that he didn't want to change.

But it would have to change in some ways as

they spent more time together, he acknowledged. Alyse had a point, even if he didn't like it.

And she seemed to want such change. Want more. Leo felt everything in him recoil at the thought. He didn't do relationships, or intimacy, or emotion, or any of it, yet it seemed Alyse expected a little of all of the above.

He could manage some conversation, he told himself. Some simple pursuits and pleasures... such as the consummation of their marriage. Perhaps he and his wife could find some sympathy with each other in bed. They certainly didn't seem to have much out of it, although he was honest enough to admit he'd never really tried.

He didn't want to get to know Alyse. He didn't want their relationship to be anything than what it was: a carefully managed façade. He never had.

Yet now it seemed she wanted something else. Something more.

Well, she wouldn't get it. He didn't have anything more to give. Suppressing a sigh, he took another sip of champagne. Why did a thought that had once comforted and strengthened him now make him only feel restless and on edge?

* * *

By the time they arrived in St Cristos, Alyse was feeling strung out and exhausted. She hated the constant tension she felt in Leo's presence; before today, they'd only seen each other for various occasions, usually formal, and always with other people around. They'd never had more than a few hours in each other's company at a time, and never more than a few minutes alone.

She had hoped that when they were alone properly things would become more natural. They would chat, get to know one another, behave like normal, civil human beings. Except civility, in Leo's world, was a cold-hearted, emotionless thing and Alyse didn't think she could take much more of it.

After their brief exchange on the jet they'd barely spoken, and they'd ridden in silence from the island's tiny airstrip to the exclusive resort. Alyse stared out of the window at the verdant hills on the horizon, the palm trees fringing the narrow track with their fronds drooping to the ground. In the distance the sea glittered under an afternoon sun; it was seven hours behind Maldinia here.

The resort came into view, a gracious grouping of thatched huts that looked both simple yet luxurious. The limo pulled to a stop and Alyse saw that all the staff was lined up outside the main hut, beaming and expectant.

She knew the resort was closed to all other guests this week in order to give her and Leo maximum privacy, yet right now she felt too tired to sparkle and charm the crowd. She wanted to curl up into herself and hide.

'Here we go,' Leo murmured, and with a rather grim smile he helped her out of the limo.

Alyse didn't remember what she said to all the people assembled; she shook hands and murmured pleasantries and Leo put his arm around her, kissing her cheek to the sighs of several chambermaids. After what felt like an hour, but was probably only a few minutes, they were led to their guest quarters in a private cove.

Alyse stood in the middle of the hut on its raised wooden platform and stared at the few, expensive furnishings: a couple of teak bureaux, a rattan chair and a huge bed with soft linen sheets. Mosquito netting was draped over the entrance, tied back now, so she had an unrestricted view of the sea lapping only a few metres away.

There were no electrical outlets, she knew, no computers, televisions, telephones or mobile reception. Nothing to keep her and Leo from spending time with one another.

Except Leo himself.

'I think I'll take a look around,' Leo said. 'Why don't you get settled?'

So much for spending time together. Alyse set about unpacking her cases, even though one of the resort staff had offered to do it for her. Right now she wanted to be alone.

Unpacking her few outfits for their week on the Caribbean island didn't take long, however, and after she'd finished she prowled restlessly around the hut, wishing Leo would return, yet half glad he hadn't. His obvious lack of interest in so much as conversing with her was hard to take.

Since Leo still wasn't around she decided to go for a swim. With a twinge of self-conscious-ness, she changed into one of the bikinis that had been selected for her; she had not chosen or even seen any of the clothes in her cases, not even the shorts and tee-shirts.

The bikini was a little more revealing than she would have liked but, shrugging aside any self-consciousness—she was alone, after all—she headed for the sea.

The sand was silky under her bare feet, the water lapping her toes clear and warm. Standing there, gazing out at an endless horizon, Alyse felt just a little of the tension she'd been carrying lessen and her shoulders relaxed a fraction.

Maybe when Leo returned they'd have that private conversation he'd resisted on the plane. She'd talk to him properly, explain that she didn't want to act like strangers any more. If they couldn't act as a normal husband and wife, at least they could be friends. Surely that would be more bearable than this horribly stilted awkwardness and avoidance?

Taking a deep breath, she dove into the water, kicking her feet as she swam several metres underwater, enjoying the freedom and the silence of the world below the waves.

When she surfaced, slicking her hair back from her face, she felt a jolt deep inside—for Leo was standing in the shallows, dressed only in board shorts as he gazed out at her.

'I wondered when you'd come back up for air,' he said, his eyes narrowed against the sun's glare. 'I didn't know you were such a good swimmer.'

She stood, for the water was still shallow there, and came up only to her waist. 'There's a lot we don't know about each other.'

Even from this distance she saw the heat flare in his eyes as his gaze roved over her bikini-clad body, rivulets of water coursing down her skin. She felt her own body react—muscles tautening, awareness firing through her, hope flaring. 'Yes,' he said slowly. 'So there is.'

Alyse's heart started thudding even as she strove to sound natural. This was the first time she'd ever seen desire in Leo's eyes, such blatant hunger. It thrilled her to the core, but it surprised and even scared her too, for there was something raw and untamed in Leo's gaze, something she'd never seen from him before. Something she'd craved. When she spoke her voice came out in a husky whisper. 'Do you want to have a swim?'

'I think I might.' He waded into the water, and her breath caught in her chest. He was so beautiful, his body hard, sculpted and *perfect*. He dove neatly into the sea, and she watched with mounting anticipation as he kicked through the water towards her, cutting through the waves to come to stand right next to her, the water lapping at his hips and running down his chest.

He was close enough to feel the heat coming off his skin, to touch him, and she longed to press her hand or even her mouth against his damp chest, to catch the droplets of water with her tongue and taste the saltiness of his skin…

Her heart felt as if it were pounding in her throat. 'It's lovely here, isn't it?' she commented, knowing she sounded inane. She didn't know how to act, what to say. All she could do was *feel*—this overwhelming desire and, even more frighteningly, hope coursing through her. Hope that, if he felt this for her, there could be more. There would be.

Yet now she couldn't think about the more, only about the now. About the reality of the desire kindling in his eyes; her breath went shallow as he lifted one hand as if he would touch her. He'd never touched her without an audience.

'It is lovely,' Leo agreed in a low voice. He reached out then and touched her cheek and, even though she'd been expecting it, craving it, the caress still caught her by surprise so her breath came out in a ragged shudder.

He stroked her cheek gently with one finger. 'You're lovely.' She stared at him, ensnared by the heat of his gaze, the touch of his hand. She saw something hard in his gaze, something cynical in his smile, and she still couldn't keep from wanting him. 'I wonder,' he mused softly, his finger still stroking her cheek, 'How do you make something that's been false, true? What's fake, real?'

Her heart seemed to burst within her like fireworks had gone off in her soul. The very fact that he was even asking the question gave her a hope that was painful in its intensity. 'I want to,' she whispered, her heart beating so hard now that it hurt, the thuds slamming her chest. 'I want this to be real, Leo.'

His lips twisted again, caught between a grimace and a smile. He bent his head, his lips a whisper away from hers. 'This is real enough,' he murmured, and then he kissed her.

It was as different from the chaste kisses he'd pressed upon her for the sake of the cameras and the crowds as could be, as she could possibly want.

His mouth slanted over hers with dark possession and he ran his tongue along the seam of her lips before he went deep into her mouth, and she gasped at the sensations scorching through her. Leo's touch felt so intensely pleasurable it was painful, as painful as the hope that still burst through her and lit her on fire.

Leo fastened his hands on her hips and fitted her against his arousal as he blazed a trail of kisses from her mouth to her cheek and jaw, and then down her neck to the vee between her breasts, his tongue licking the salt from her skin. Alyse shuddered and tilted her head back, allowing him greater access to her body, to everything in her.

'Leo...'

He lifted his head, gave her one of his cool smiles. 'This has all got a bit out of control, hasn't it? I don't want to have our wedding night right here in the sea.' He stepped away and Alyse felt a sudden rush of cold emptiness. 'In any case, I only came to find you and tell you dinner will be served shortly. The staff of the resort are setting up a table here on the beach.'

Alyse's mind was spinning, the hope draining

out of her, leaving nothing but that aching, pulsing need. Somehow she forced herself to sound as unconcerned, as unaffected as he seemed to be. 'We could eat in the restaurant.'

'Ah, but this is more romantic.'

Alyse watched Leo swim back to the beach and with a deep, shuddering breath, willing her wayward body back under control, she dove underwater and started back towards the shore.

As soon as he reached their hut, Leo grabbed his clothes and headed for the shower. He needed a cold one. He hadn't meant lust to overtake him quite so much when he'd joined Alyse in the water, but the sight of her barely clad body had driven all rational thought from his mind. He'd been waiting a long time for his body's basic needs to be fulfilled, and the kiss he'd shared with her had been surprisingly sweet.

No, not sweet—hungry, demanding and raw. It had awakened a deeper need in him than he'd ever acknowledged before, and it had taken nearly all of his willpower to step away from her. She was surely a virgin, and he knew she deserved more than a fumbled grope on the sand. He wanted to take his time, bring them both pleasure and not just release. That was one area of their marriage where, he hoped, they could both find some kind of happiness.

Still, he didn't like how close he'd come to losing control there in the water. He never lost control, never even let it slip—and the last person he wanted to weaken him in that area was his wife.

By the time he'd spent ten minutes in an icy shower he felt his composure return and his libido calm down. He changed into a fresh pair of chinos and a dark green polo shirt, and headed back to their hut.

Alyse had already showered in a separate bathroom and was sitting in a rattan chair, her hair damp and curling about her shoulders. She wore a floaty blue sundress that brought out the blue in her eyes, her legs tanned and endless, her feet bare.

Every time he'd seen Alyse she'd been surrounded by stylists, her clothes carefully chosen, her make-up perfectly done, not a hair out of place. Now he saw her face was make-up-free and the sun had already caused a few freckles to appear on the bridge of her nose. She looked better like this, he decided. More natural. He wondered if she missed all the primping and attention, if she enjoyed the clothes, make-up and jewels.

He didn't know, and decided not to ask. He didn't need to know. He didn't want to care.

Yet even so he couldn't suppress the flicker of interest—and, yes, desire—this new, natural Alyse stirred within him.

The sun was just starting to set, sending long, golden rays across the placid surface of the sea, and Leo could see the staff already setting up their romantic table for two there on the beach. He busied himself unpacking his things while Alyse read, conscious of her nearness, the warmth and softness of her, and even the subtle floral scent of her shampoo or perfume, something he'd never even noticed before.

Even now he remembered the feel of her lips on his, the lush softness of her mouth, her breasts, the hunger of her response. His libido stirred insistently and he blew out an impatient breath. *Control.*

'Dinner's ready,' he said more brusquely than

he intended, and nodded towards the table now laid for two on the sand.

Alyse looked up from her e-reader and, tossing it aside, rose from her chair. The sundress she wore clung to her figure, highlighting the small yet perfect roundness of her breasts, her tiny waist, her endless legs. Even though she was thinner than she probably should have been—no doubt due to the stress of the run-up to the wedding—she still had a lovely figure, an amazing figure, and Leo's palms itched to touch her. His body stirred again, insistent, demanding.

Tonight, he decided. They would make their marriage real tonight—real in the only way that mattered, the only way possible.

In bed.

CHAPTER FOUR

ALYSE FOLLOWED LEO out onto the beach, a violet twilight settling all around them as the sun started to slip beneath the sea.

The staff who had set up their table had all melted away, so they were alone with the flickering candlelight, a bucket on the sand with champagne chilling, the first course of crab salad already laid out on exquisite porcelain plates. It was the most romantic dinner Alyse ever could have imagined…and it felt like a minefield.

She had no idea how to act with Leo, especially after that kiss. Already she'd spent far too long reliving it—surely the most wonderful kiss she'd ever known—and thrilling to the undeniable realisation that Leo desired her.

How do you make something that's been false, true? His words had buoyed her soul at that moment, because in all her naïve hope she'd thought he meant their relationship. Their marriage.

This is real.

Watching Leo stride along the shore away from her, Alyse had known then what he'd really meant: the only real thing between them was sexual attraction.

Still, it's something, she told herself as she followed Leo out onto the twilit beach. *It might grow into more.* But only if given a chance…a chance Leo seemed determined not to take.

With a little bow, he pulled out her chair and Alyse sat down. 'Wine?' he asked, and she nodded.

He poured them both glasses and then sat across from her, sipping his wine as he gazed out at the sea, its surface now the inky violet of twilight.

He might not be willing to take that chance, she acknowledged, but she had to be. Taking a deep breath, Alyse gave him as bright a smile as she could manage. 'So, what should we do tomorrow? Snorkel? Scuba? Hike?'

His eyebrows rose, his expression freezing for a second, so she almost laughed. 'Don't look so terrified,' she said dryly, parroting his words from last night back at him. 'I might have suggested macramé.'

'Macramé? I'm not even sure what that is.'

'Weaving with knots,' Alyse explained. 'It's one of my passions. I was hoping you might share it.' Leo looked so nonplussed that this time she did laugh, and the release felt good. Even better was his answering rasp of a chuckle.

'You're having me on.' He shook his head, taking a sip of wine. 'Six years and I had no idea you had a sense of humour.'

Because he'd never had the chance to find out, or the desire. 'Well, we've never had a proper conversation before, not really,' Alyse said. She was trying for light but her voice came out quiet, almost forlorn. She'd have to do better. 'Not one about macramé, at any rate.'

'I must admit, I'm relieved it isn't one of your passions,' Leo answered. He arched an eyebrow, and she was gratified by the lightness of his expression. 'It isn't, is it?'

'No.' A smile twitched at her mouth. 'Definitely not one of them.' Leo just nodded, and despite the obvious opening Alyse knew he wasn't going to press. He would never press, never ask her about herself, what her passions or even her hobbies were. 'So, scuba, then?' she said, keeping her voice bright. 'I'm not qualified, but I read that they have instructors here who can qualify you with a day course.'

Leo made a noncommittal noise and Alyse felt the hurt and anger return, filling the empty places inside her. 'I think you'd enjoy scuba diving,' she said, and heard a new sharp note enter her voice. 'It doesn't allow for any conversation.'

'I have nothing against conversation.'

'Conversation with *me*, then?'

He shook his head, annoyance sparking in his eyes. 'Alyse...'

'I just don't see,' she pressed on in a desperate rush, knowing she needed to say it, to get it out there, 'why we can't be friends. Our marriage is unconventional, I know. I accept that. But we have to live together, Leo. We have to have a life together of some description. And I would like to do that as—as your friend.'

Silence. Leo said nothing, just eyed her over the rim of his wine glass. Why, Alyse wondered, did such a benign offer of friendship make her feel so vulnerable? So needy and demanding?

Because Leo obviously didn't need anyone, and certainly not her. Not even as a friend.

'Say something,' she finally said, just to break the awful silence.

'I don't know what I could say that you'd wish to hear.'

'At this point, anything is better than nothing,' she answered tartly.

'I'm not sure it's possible,' Leo said, each word chosen carefully, 'for us to be friends.'

'Not possible?' She stared at him in confusion. 'Why?'

'Because,' Leo replied, his voice still so terribly careful, 'I have no wish to be friends with you.'

As soon as he said the words, Leo realised how cruel they sounded. Cruel and deliberately cold... and he hadn't meant it quite like that. Had he?

From the moment Alyse had started teasing and tempting him in turns—asking for things he didn't know how to give—he hadn't known what he meant. How he felt.

And as for the look on Alyse's face... She looked stunned for a moment, and then he saw a flash of hurt darken her eyes before she turned her face away, her expression hidden in the dark.

'Alyse…' he said, although he had no idea how to explain himself, or even if he could. In any case, he didn't get a chance.

With a small sound of distress she rose from the table and walked quickly across the beach, her slight form soon swallowed up by darkness.

Irritation mixed uncomfortably with an already increasing guilt—and a wretched sense of disappointment in himself. He should have handled that better. He should have known how.

He threw his napkin down and rose, his hands braced flat on the table. 'Where are you going?' he called, and from the twilit shadows he heard her muffled response.

'If you're worried I'm going to do something indiscreet, never fear. I just couldn't bear sitting at the table with you.'

His lips twitched with a sudden, macabre humour. 'I'm not surprised.' She didn't answer and he sighed wearily. 'I can't even see you,' he said, taking a few steps towards her. The sand was cool and silky under his bare feet. 'Where are you hiding?'

'I'm not *hiding*,' she snapped, and as he moved closer to the sound of her voice he saw she'd gone to the far side of the little cove, her back to him and the sea as she stood facing the rocky outcropping, her shoulders hunched, her arms wrapped around herself. There wasn't really anywhere else for her to go.

'I'm sorry,' he said after a moment. 'That came out wrong.'

'Was there really room for misinterpretation?'

'I only meant I think it would be easier if we didn't attempt to be friends.'

She let out a harsh bark of disbelieving laughter and turned around. 'Easier? For you, maybe.'

'Yes, for me.' He shifted his weight, his hands digging into his pockets. 'I don't think I need to remind you that this marriage was never meant to be anything but a matter of convenience, Alyse. A business deal.'

'That doesn't mean it can't become something else,' she said quietly. 'Something more.'

Something more? Even though he'd begun to suspect she harboured such hopes, the possibility still appalled him.

'Clearly you find that notion horrifying,' she continued, a hint of mockery in her voice. 'I've reduced you to silence.'

'It's unexpected,' he answered carefully. 'I've thought we've been in agreement about what our marriage would look like.'

'Considering we never discussed it, I don't know how we could be, or why you would think so.'

'Considering we both agreed to play-act at a relationship for six whole years,' he retorted, 'I'm not sure why you think it would suddenly change now, or why either of us would want it to.' He stared at her, her chin tilted in determination or maybe even defiance, her eyes sparking silver. Frustration flared within him; this was so *unexpected*. And he hated how it made him feel—cornered, angry and, damn it, uncertain. He'd been so sure about what he wanted—and what he didn't want.

Why was this woman he'd thought he knew so well—that was, not at all—changing and, far more alarmingly, making him change?

He straightened, arms folded. 'We both got what we wanted out of this union, Alyse.'

She lifted her chin a notch. 'Which is?'

'To restore the monarchy's reputation and provide an heir.'

'Ah, an heir.' She folded her arms, mirroring his own implacable stance, and stared him down. 'And sex with you is such an appealing prospect, considering you just told me you have no interest at all in getting to know me.'

'I don't know why it would make a difference,' he answered coolly, and she let out a high, wild laugh.

'I should have known you'd say something like that.'

Leo raked a hand through his hair. He needed to perform some damage control, and quickly. 'Look, I told you, I didn't mean it quite like it sounded. I just never thought about—about friendship.'

'Actually, I think you did mean it. You just didn't mean for it to sound as brutal as it really is.' She walked past him back to their table, her dress nearly brushing his legs, and he inhaled the scent of sunshine and sea as she passed.

After a moment Leo followed her back to the table; she'd sat down and was eating her salad with a methodical diligence that suggested no enjoyment in the food at all.

Leo sat down as well, although his appetite had,

annoyingly, vanished. Gazing at her pale, drawn face, he still felt guilty, as if he'd disappointed or even hurt her somehow. It was a feeling he'd experienced in varying degrees since they'd said their marriage vows, and he didn't like it.

He didn't want her to be hurt, and more to the point he didn't want to care if she was. Yet somehow he knew both were true, and he wasn't sure what to do about it.

'I honestly didn't mean to offend you,' he finally said, his tone terse, when Alyse had ploughed through half her salad. His remained untouched.

'I suggest we be friends and you say you have no interest in such a thing,' she returned, not even looking up from her food. 'How is that not going to be offensive?'

'You took me by surprise,' he snapped, goaded into revealing a temper he'd barely known he had. 'For six years we've been as strangers to each other, and you seemed fine with that. Why should I expect anything to change now?'

'Because we're *married.*'

'It's nothing more than a promise and a piece of paper,' Leo said brutally, his temper now well and truly lit. 'It doesn't actually change anything. It doesn't have to.'

She looked up then, her face pale, her lush mouth bloodless. 'Because you don't want anything to change.'

'No, I don't.'

She shook her head slowly, biting those bloodless lips as she looked away. 'Why not?' she asked softly. 'What do you have against me?'

'Oh, for...' He sighed wearily. 'Nothing. I don't have anything against you.'

'Just women in general, then?'

Leo suppressed a curse. 'No, I have no problem with women, Alyse. I don't have a problem with anything. I simply want what I thought we'd agreed on all those years ago—a relationship of convenience, managed and manufactured for the sake of restoring the monarchy.'

'Do you really think I care about the monarchy?' she asked, her voice turning ragged with emotion, reminding him of ripped and ruined things, things torn by desire and broken by need.

He'd felt it once in himself, long ago, that endless ache of disappointment and sorrow. He intended never to feel it again, and he certainly didn't want it coming from his wife. The whole *point* of this marriage had been to avoid such messiness, such pain. That was the benefit of pretending, never mind the cost.

'I suppose you care,' Leo answered evenly. 'Since you agreed to marry me and perpetuate this charade.'

She glanced away, and in the darkness he could not make out her expression at all. 'I've never cared about the monarchy. Or being queen. Or—any of it.'

The bleakness of her tone had the hairs on the back of his neck prickling. He believed her, and he didn't want to. It would be much simpler to believe she'd agreed to their arrangement because of the material benefits she'd enjoy. *So much sim pler.* 'Then why did you agree to a pretend engagement? A pretend marriage?' he asked, the words drawn from him reluctantly. It was a question he'd never asked her, never wanted to ask her. It had been enough that she'd accepted. Now, with an increasing sense of foreboding, he braced himself for her answer.

'Why?' Alyse repeated, and her voice sounded

far away, her face still averted. She let out a long, shuddering breath. 'It doesn't really matter now.'

And, even though he knew that was no answer at all, Leo chose not to press. He really didn't want to know.

Neither of them spoke for a long moment, the silence strained and somehow sad. Then Alyse turned to him, her expression carefully veiled, yet Leo still felt the hurt emanating from her. It exasperated him, how much he felt now, both from her and in himself. For years he'd managed perfectly well, not feeling anything. Not wanting to.

'I still don't see how friendship will complicate things,' she said quietly. 'I would have thought it would make things easier. We're going to spend the rest of our lives together, after all. We are, God willing, going to have children—' She broke off suddenly, her voice having turned ragged again, and he could feel the need pulsing through her.

That was why friendship would complicate things—because it would open a door he'd kept firmly and forever shut. 'You knew all this before, Alyse,' he said. 'You knew what you were getting into. What you were agreeing to.'

'Knowing something and actually living it are two different things.' She shook her head slowly. 'Do you really not feel any differently, Leo? That actually being married makes a difference?'

He wanted to say no. He should say no, and nip all this talk of friendship and feelings in the bud. Yet he couldn't because, damn it, he did feel differently. He just didn't want to.

Impatiently, he tossed his napkin on the table. He'd barely touched his meal, but he wasn't hungry. 'Look,' he said flatly. 'The reason I said what I said is because I'm not sure I can even be your friend.'

'Why?'

'Because I don't— I've never really had a friend before.' That sounded so utterly pathetic, he realised furiously. He hated, *hated* that she'd driven him to such a confession.

Alyse gaped at him, her jaw dropping inelegantly. 'You've never had a friend?' she said in disbelief, and Leo felt his own jaw bunch, teeth grating.

'Not really.' He was lying, though. He'd had

one friend at least—the best friend and brother whom he'd loved more than anyone else. The one person he'd been real with, the one person he'd trusted.

And look how that had turned out. The most real relationship he'd ever had had turned out to be as fake as all the others.

'Why not?' she asked and he just shrugged. She waited: a stand-off.

'When you live your life under the microscope, genuine friendship isn't easy to come by,' he finally said, his voice brusque. *When you lived your life in the spotlight. When the only time anyone was interested in affection or emotion was for the cameras...*

He wasn't about to explain all that. How could he? He'd hated the glare of the spotlight, yet he'd chosen it for himself and his marriage. Willingly...because at least then he was in control.

Yet he didn't feel much in control at the moment. He felt as if it had been slipping away from him ever since he'd stood next to Alyse in the cathedral and said those vows.

'Even so,' she said, and he heard damnable pity

in her voice. 'I would have thought there would be someone—'

'I haven't lived in complete isolation.' He cut her off, his voice coming out in something close to a snap. 'I've had acquaintances, servants, staff...'

'It's not the same.'

'Probably not. But you don't miss what you've never had.' Except he'd had it, and he knew he would miss it if he let himself—which he never did.

Alyse was silent for a long moment. Her expression had turned thoughtful, her head tilted to one side as her quiet gaze swept over him. Leo felt as if he were under a searchlight. 'Do you think,' she finally asked, 'you might be willing to try with me?'

'Try what?'

'Being my friend. Letting me be yours.'

Leo felt his jaw bunch harder and he wiped a hand over his face. 'Next we'll be painting each other's nails and doing—what was it?—macramé?'

A tiny smile hovered on Alyse's lush mouth and despite all the wretched emotion between them Leo felt his libido kick in hard. 'I promise, no weaving. Or nail varnish.'

'Right.' He tried to smile in response but somehow he couldn't. He couldn't take any more of this: not the emotion, not the honesty, not the damn intimacy. He felt as if he was going to burst out of his skin.

He turned resolutely back to his meal. 'Snorkelling sounds like a plan,' he said gruffly. Just as Alyse had said, you couldn't talk with a tube in your mouth. And, from the way her mouth turned down at the corners, Leo had a feeling she'd guessed the exact nature of his thoughts.

CHAPTER FIVE

As SOON AS they'd finished eating, Leo excused himself to go for a walk. Alyse watched him head down the beach into the darkness with a tired sigh. She didn't ask to join him, knew he'd had enough. Their conversation tonight had been more honest and intimate than anything they'd shared in the last six years, yet it just made her realise how little they actually had. How little they knew each other.

And yet she loved him. How could you love someone you barely knew, someone who purposely kept himself hidden from you and everyone?

It was a question she'd asked herself many times, and with no real answer, and yet she'd never been able to deny or suppress the hopeless longing he made her feel, and had done from the moment he'd come to her eighteenth birthday party. How the sight of one of his rare smiles had made her heart soar, and the barest brush of his fingers had made it leap. She didn't understand why, but she recognized the signs. Just like her parents had.

Love at first sight, and she wouldn't wish it on anyone—at least not when it wasn't returned.

Sighing again, she headed back to their hut. It was the middle of the night in Maldinian time, and she was utterly exhausted.

Yet as she lay between the cool linen sheets and waited for Leo to return, listening to the waves washing onto the sound and the soothing chirrup of the cicadas, sleep continued to elude her. Her body still felt tense, her mind still racing as it replayed tonight's conversation with Leo.

I've never really had a friend before.

Had he meant that literally? How was it possible? Yet if he'd spoken the truth—which she believed he had—then it explained so much. His cool containment, his preference for his own company. His lack of desire for anything intimate, honest or real.

Her own childhood had, in a way, been similarly lonely. She was an only child of parents who had been rather rapturously wrapped up in each other. She'd been tutored by a taciturn governess and then sent to a boarding school where she'd been too shy ever to feel as if she really fit in. At university she'd made friends, at least—*and look where that had led her.*

And then of course the last six years in the public eye… Sometimes the connection she'd experienced with the people who thronged the streets to greet her felt like the most real, honest human interaction in her life, which certainly said something about the lack of real intimacy in her own life.

Strange to think both she and Leo had experienced such loneliness, yet they'd reacted to it in completely different ways. He embraced isolation; she craved closeness.

She wondered if they would ever find a way to compromise, and if such a thing could satisfy either of them.

Leo walked as far down the beach as he could, before a jagged outcropping of rocks stopped his path. He stopped and let out a weary sigh. After the excruciating intimacy of his conversation with Alyse, he'd needed space. Escape.

But, standing here looking at the rocky barrier, he knew he couldn't outrun his thoughts.

She was asking for something so little, he knew. Something so reasonable: friendship. Friendship wasn't meant to be threatening or scary. It could, in fact, make things easier, just as she'd said. Certainly getting along with one another was better than existing in cold silence, and yet...

His whole life had been about cold silence. About work and duty and *doing*, because those things didn't let you down. Didn't hurt you. They were steady, safe.

And friendship might seem innocent, innocuous, but Leo knew how opening your heart just a little could still allow the pain and need to rush in. And, in any case, he didn't even know how to be a friend. Maybe it seemed incredible and, yes, pathetic, but it was the truth.

He'd lived a solitary life for so long and he didn't want to change.

Yet already, inexorably, impossibly, he felt himself changing. Already he was wondering just how badly he'd hurt her feelings tonight, and hating that he had. Hating even more that he cared that he had.

That's not what this marriage was meant to be about.

Cursing under his breath, he whirled around and began to stride back to the hut.

By the time he returned Alyse was in bed, her slight form draped with the linen sheet. She lay flat on her back, staring at the ceiling and not moving at all.

Leo came in and sat on the edge of the bed. He felt almost unbearably tired, not just from the long flight and the jet lag but from the unexpected roller coaster of emotions they'd both ridden on since their wedding, all of it too much, more than he'd felt in years.

'Are you awake?' he asked quietly and he heard Alyse exhale.

'Funnily enough, I can't get to sleep.'

He half-turned towards her, trying to make out her expression in the moonlit darkness and unable to. 'It's not just an out-of-sync body clock, I suppose?'

She let out a little huff that almost sounded like a laugh and amazingly, absurdly, Leo felt his heart lighten. 'Unfortunately not.'

She shifted in the bed, and he saw the slinky

strap of her nightgown fall from one shoulder. His gaze was drawn inexorably to the smooth skin of her neck, her shoulder, and then downwards to the warm curve of her breast. Despite the tension that still vibrated between them, he felt the insistent stirring of arousal. He forced himself to look up into her eyes, and saw she was watching him with a wary expectation.

'I'm sorry,' he said.

'For what, exactly?' He heard a thread of humour in her voice and to his surprise he found himself matching it.

'It must be really bad, if there are options. Have you compiled a list?'

'That sounds like something you would do.'

He let out a tired huff of laughter and raked his hand through his hair. 'Yours is probably a lot longer than mine.'

'Maybe not,' she said softly, and something in him twisted. Yearned.

'I'm sorry for the way I handled our conversation,' he clarified gruffly, pushing away that strange yearning. 'And the unkind things I said to you. They were neither appropriate nor necessary.'

'That's a very formal apology.'

He bristled, instinctively, helplessly. 'I don't know any other way.'

She sighed. 'It's all right, Leo. I accept your apology.' She hesitated, and he heard the gentle in and out of her breath, saw the rise and fall of her chest in the moonlight, her breasts barely covered by a scrap of silky negligee. Had she not packed *any* decent pyjamas?

Of course she hadn't. This was their honeymoon, and they were meant to be wildly in love.

'What now?' she asked after a moment, and he watched as she picked at a thread in the linen sheet with slender, elegant fingers. 'Do you think we can be friends?'

'I can try,' Leo answered, the words drawn from him reluctantly. He hated how weak he sounded. How…incapable. But the truth was trying was all he could do, and he didn't even know if he could do that very well.

Alyse glanced up at him, blinking in the moonlit darkness, a small, wry smile curving her lips. 'I can't ask for more than that.'

'I still want what I wanted before,' Leo told

her gruffly, the words a warning. 'A business arrangement, a marriage of convenience.'

Her smile faltered slightly and she glanced away before she met his gaze once more. 'Business arrangements don't have to be cold-blooded. Emotionless.'

Oh yes, they did. For him. Because that was who he was, who he'd determined to be, how to act. Not to feel. Not to want. Not to be disappointed or hurt.

'They can be friendly,' Alyse continued, her voice holding a hint of humour, of hope. And he wondered just what she was hoping for. How much.

Sighing, he pulled his shirt off and reached for his pyjamas. He changed quickly, conscious of Alyse so close to him, and the fact that despite the rather abhorrent intimacy of their conversation, they still hadn't been physically intimate yet. And, hell if he knew now when they would be. Sex and emotion did *not* go together. Yet after tonight he had a feeling Alyse wouldn't be able to separate them. The last thing he needed was her wanting something more than friendship—something ridiculous, like love.

'Look,' he said as he slid between the sheets, knowing he needed to be completely clear, 'I'm not going to love you. I don't love anyone and I never have.'

She was silent for a long moment. 'Is that what you're worried about?' she asked eventually. 'That, in becoming friends, I might fall in love with you?'

'You might convince yourself you are.'

'You make me sound deluded.'

'Anyone who believes in love is deluded,' Leo said flatly, and he felt Alyse shift next to him, turning to face him.

'Deluded? Why do you think that?'

'Because love isn't real,' Leo stated. 'It's just a hormonal urge, a feeling that changes depending on your mood. It's certainly nothing I've ever pursued or even believed in.'

She was silent for so long Leo, annoyingly, felt a little self-conscious, as if he'd said something he shouldn't have. Revealed more about himself than he'd ever wanted to.

'If you don't think love is even real,' Alyse finally said, 'then you don't need to worry about me feeling it, do you?'

He sighed, shifting away from her tempting warmth. 'I just want to be clear about our expectations. I'm willing to try and be friends, of a sort, but that's all.'

'Of a sort?' She was trying once more for humour but he heard the hurt underneath the wryness. 'What sort is that, Leo?'

He stared up at the ceiling, the ocean breeze causing the palm fronds of the hut to rustle and sway. 'I told you, I haven't had many friends. I'll do my best.'

She turned towards him, and he felt her breasts brush his shoulder. Instantly he was hard. 'That's all anybody can do, isn't it? Your best.'

He breathed in the fresh, floral scent of her and his whole body pulsed with longing. As carefully as he could he moved away from her softness. Sex, he knew, was out of the question for tonight. But soon, damn it. *Very soon*. 'As long as being friends—of a sort—is enough for you,' he answered grudgingly and even through the darkness he saw and felt her sad smile.

'I suppose it will have to be,' she said, and then neither of them spoke again.

CHAPTER SIX

ALYSE WOKE TO the warm spill of sunshine and the gentle *swooshing* of the waves just metres from their bed. She turned to see Leo still asleep next to her, one hand flung over his head, the dark glint of morning stubble visible on his jaw. His lashes, surprisingly long, feathered his cheeks and those all-too-kissable lips were slightly parted. He looked gentler, somehow, in sleep. Softer, almost vulnerable, and so different from the cold, hard man he seemed when he was awake.

She let her gaze move lower and took in his bare chest, the rise and fall of it with each steady breath. Lower still, to the sheet rucked about his waist, his legs tangled beneath it.

Her mouth dried and for a few more seconds she tortured herself by drinking in the male perfection of his body without him knowing. Her gaze was lingering, longing, and completely unrestrained. How would it feel to touch that chest, to slide her hand from shoulder to hip and feel the hot satin of his skin under her seeking fingers?

Desire spiralled dizzily inside her. Never mind wanting to be friends; she just wanted him. For a brief moment she toyed with the idea of touching him. Kissing him awake. But she knew she wasn't bold enough, was too afraid of his surprise or even rejection.

Yet when would they consummate this marriage? When would friendship and desire meld, if ever?

And dared she still hope for more?

Silently she slid from the bed and reached for the robe that matched her nightgown, yet another ridiculous, silky confection. With one last look at Leo, who still seemed deeply asleep, she slipped out of the hut.

The day was already warm although Alyse suspected it wasn't much past dawn, the sun having only just risen over the horizon, its golden light pooling on the placid surface of the sea.

She sat on the beach, tucking her robe around her, and sifted the sun-warmed sand through her fingers as last night's conversation swirled through her mind: Leo's confession that he hadn't had any friends, his grudging acceptance that they might be friends—*of a sort*—and his flat and absolute statement that he would never love her.

Could she really be surprised by that bleak statement? It was no more than what she'd suspected, feared, and had tried to convince herself to believe over the years. And yet…she *had* believed in the miracle. The possibility of a miracle. She'd lied to Leo last night about that, just as she'd lied to herself over the last six years. She'd clung, stubbornly and stupidly, to the hope that he would learn to love her. That things would somehow miraculously change.

And she still clung to it now. Alyse's mouth twisted in a grim smile as she acknowledged the truth. Despite everything Leo had said, she still hoped he might come to love her in time, that physical attraction and possible friendship might deepen into the kind of love he didn't even believe in.

The smarter thing to do would be to let go of that hope, let it trickle away like water in sand, and get on with what was possible. Alyse knew she wouldn't. Couldn't. She'd keep hoping, keep believing, because thin vapour that it was, hope was all that sustained her.

And why shouldn't Leo love her? Why shouldn't it be possible, eventually, ultimately?

I'm not going to love you. I don't love anyone and I never have. The memory of his words made her both wince and wonder. Why didn't he love anyone, not even his parents or his sister? *Anyone who believes in love is deluded.* And what had made him lock up his heart so coldly and tightly that he refused even to believe love could exist, never mind flourish?

Could she—did she dare—be the one to try and unlock it?

'Good morning.'

Alyse turned to see Leo standing on the beach just a little bit away from her. He still wore only his pyjama bottoms and he looked glorious. She hoped her recent thoughts weren't visible on her face, her contrary hope reflected in her eyes.

'Good morning.'

'Did you sleep well?'

'Not particularly.'

He smiled then, a proper grin that set her heart

racing. Did he know how attractive he was, how a single smile made her heart turn somersaults and then soar straight up into the sky?

'Me neither.' Leo came to sit beside her, stretching his legs out alongside hers. 'I'm not used to conversations like last night's.'

'I gathered that.'

'It was rather obvious, wasn't it?'

His wry smile tugged at her heart. 'Considering revealing anything of a personal nature seems to be akin to pulling teeth for you, I'd say yes.'

He chuckled softly and shook his head. 'Well. I tried.'

'That's all I'm asking for.'

He turned to her then, his gaze dark and searching, his smile gone. 'Is it?'

She fell silent under that searching and seemingly knowing gaze, for of course it wasn't—and it seemed he knew that, or at least suspected. Did he guess that she was in love with him? The possibility made both humiliation and hope rush through her.

She wanted him to know her feelings, wanted to stop pretending, and yet…the thought of his contempt and horror made everything inside her shrivel. She couldn't risk revealing so much. Not yet, and maybe not ever.

'So, snorkelling,' he said, and she nodded.

'Sounds fun.'

'Why don't we get dressed and go for breakfast, and then we can sort it out after?'

'All right.'

With a brisk nod Leo rose from the sand, brushing off his pyjamas, and headed back to the hut. Alyse watched him go, half-amazed that she was finally, actually going to spend an entire day in Leo's company… And still, as always, hopeful for what this day might bring.

This friendship business, Leo decided, was simple. At least so far. All he had to do was spend a little time with Alyse, *do* things with her. That suited him; he preferred having a plan, preferred action to talking. As long as they kept it to leisure activities, preferably ones that kept them from conversing, he'd be fine. Everything would be fine. The thought brought him a rush of much-needed relief.

Twenty minutes later they were both dressed and heading over to the main resort for breakfast. Alyse wore a pair of body-hugging canvas shorts that made Leo even more aware of her long, slim legs and the curve of her bottom. The tee-shirt she wore, in a pale petal-pink, seemed tight to Leo. Not obscenely so, but he kept finding his gaze being drawn to the high, firm breasts he'd seen on such provocative display in those frothy nightgowns she wore. Her hair was loose and fell down her back in shining, dark waves and her eyes sparkled silver as she fell into step beside him.

He'd always thought her pretty enough but now, seeing her looking natural rather than coiffed, styled and professionally made up, he realised she was actually quite beautiful.

And he wanted her very badly.

There was no reason, he thought, why they couldn't be friends by day and lovers by night. Really, it was the perfect solution.

As long as Alyse didn't confuse the two. As long as she didn't start wanting more.

He'd just have to make sure she didn't.

The restaurant, of course, was empty except for half a dozen staff who scurried to attention as soon as Leo and Alyse entered the pavilion that was shaded from the sun and open to the sea.

They sat at a table in the corner and soon had a pot of coffee and a pitcher of freshly squeezed orange juice in front of them.

'I'm starving,' Alyse confessed. She glanced at the buffet that was spread out along one side of the pavilion. 'I think there's plenty of food.'

Leo followed her gaze, taking in the platters of pastries and bowls of fresh fruit, the personal chef on hand to make omelettes to order and the several silver tureens of bacon, sausage and eggs. 'So it seems.'

'It's a bit of a waste, though, isn't it?' she said. 'When we're the only ones staying here.'

'I'm sure the staff will eat it. The resort is meant to be eco-friendly.'

'That's good to know.' She looked at him curiously. 'Are you very concerned about such things?'

He shrugged. 'I certainly intend to bring my country into the twenty-first century, in environmental matters as well as in others.'

He saw the curiosity flare in her eyes. 'Others? What kinds of things?'

He shrugged again, discomfited now. He wasn't used to talking about himself. He wasn't used to anyone asking. 'Technologically, Maldinia is about twenty years behind the rest of Europe. I've been drafting a proposal for broadband to be accessible to most areas.'

'Is it not now?'

'Really just in Averne and the outlying towns and tourist resorts. Admittedly, most of Maldinia is agricultural, and their methods are about a hundred years out of date, never mind twenty.'

She smiled, her eyes lightening with humour. 'But that must be good for the tourist revenue—very quaint, those farmers in traditional dress herding their sheep along with their wooden crooks.'

He acknowledged the point with a wry nod. 'They do look rather nice on a postcard. But those farmers should be able to check the weather—or the latest football scores—on the Internet when they get back home, don't you think?'

She laughed, the sound silvery and crystal-clear. It was a sound, Leo realised with a jolt, that he liked to hear, and he hadn't heard it very much over the last six years. 'Absolutely. Internet access is practically an inalienable right these days.'

'Inalienable,' he agreed solemnly, and they smiled at each other, the moment spinning out first in simple enjoyment and then in something Leo didn't quite recognise. Something that didn't just skim the surface of his feelings but dove deeper, surprising and almost hurting him with its strange poignancy.

Alyse looked away first. 'I didn't realise you were already involved in governing your country.'

Leo's mouth tightened, the moment evaporating like so much morning mist, gone with the first glare of light. *Good.* It was better that way. 'A bit,' he answered, his tone instinctively repressive.

He wasn't involved, not as much as he wanted to be. He'd been trying to prove to his father for fifteen years that he was capable of being king. That he deserved responsibility and respect. King Alessandro might not be interested in government policy—he was too absorbed in his own selfish pleasures for that—but he didn't want his son cramping his style or seizing his power.

He'd never wanted him to be king at all, and even after a decade and a half as heir Leo never forgot he was second choice. Second best.

Alyse stirred her coffee, her gaze thoughtful. 'There's so much I don't know about you,' she said, and the ensuing, expectant pause made Leo tense. Spending time together was one thing. You couldn't talk while you were snorkelling. But getting to know each other…having Alyse ask him questions…having to answer them… That was an entirely different prospect.

'Don't look so horrified,' she continued dryly. 'I'm not about to ask you for your deepest, darkest secrets.'

'I don't have any secrets. Not too many, anyway.' He tried to speak lightly, but he felt unsettled, uneasy, because for a few moments he'd enjoyed their conversation—the light banter, as well as, God help him, the deeper discussion—and *that* horrified him more than anything Alyse could ask.

Well, almost.

'So no embarrassing moments?' she quipped, a smile on the lips Leo kept realising were incredibly lush and kissable. He remembered how they had tasted. How *she'd* tasted. Honey-sweet with a tang of salt from the sea. Amazing. 'No secret fears?'

He forced his gaze away from her mouth, up towards her eyes that sparkled with humour. How had he never noticed how silver her eyes were? They weren't grey at all. They were warm and soft, glinting with golden lights, like a moonlit, starry sky…

Good Lord. He was thinking like some sort of besotted fool. Eyes couldn't be *soft*, and he wasn't about to compare them to the night sky.

What was *happening* to him?

'Secret fears?' he repeated, forcing his attention back to the conversation. 'No, I don't have any of those.' None he was willing to share, anyway, and he wouldn't exactly call them *fears*. More like…concerns.

'Oh come on, Leo. There must be something.'

'Why don't you tell me something about you?' he suggested. 'Most embarrassing moment or secret fear or…I don't know…funny dream.'

Her mouth curved wider and she leaned forward. 'Here's something you don't know.'

'Very well.' There had to be a thousand things

he didn't know about her, but he felt a sudden, sharp curiosity to hear this one and he leaned forward too.

'That kiss? The photo that started it all?'

'Yes.'

'I only clasped your cheek because I was wearing high heels for the first time and I was about to lose my balance.'

Leo stared at her for a moment, nonplussed, almost disbelieving, and then he burst into laughter. She grinned back and then she started laughing too, and from the corner of his eye he could see several members of the restaurant staff beaming in approval.

This would make a good photo.

The thought was enough to sober him up completely. 'And to think,' he said just a little too flatly, 'if you'd been wearing flats we might not even be married.'

'No,' Alyse agreed, all traces of laughter gone from her face. 'We might not be.' They stared at each other for a moment, and this time Leo felt a certain bleakness in their shared look. Their engagement—their whole lives, entwined as they were—had hinged on something so trivial. So ridiculous.

Why did the thought—which wouldn't have bothered him a bit before; hell, he'd have appreciated the irony—make him feel almost *sad* now? Sad not just for himself but for Alyse, for the way her eyes shuttered and her mouth twisted, and the warmth and ease they'd been sharing seemed to disappear completely.

He needed to put a stop to this somehow. He needed to stop wondering, stop *feeling* so damn much. The trouble was, he didn't know how to stop it. And, worse, part of him didn't even want to.

Alyse knew she shouldn't be hurt by Leo's observation. It was no more than the truth, the truth she'd known all along. Yet the reminder stung, when for the first time they'd actually seemed to be enjoying each other's company.

Not wanting Leo to see how absurdly hurt she felt, she rose from the table and headed for the buffet, filling her plate up with a variety of tempting items. Leo followed, and by the time they were both back at the table her composure was firmly restored.

'So,' she said, spearing a piece of papaya, 'your turn. Secret fear, embarrassing moment, funny dream. Take your pick.'

'I don't have any of those,' Leo answered. She watched him neatly break a croissant in two and rolled her eyes.

'Come on, Leo. You're not a robot. You're a man with feelings and thoughts, hopes and fears. You're *human*. Aren't you? Or am I going to roll over in bed one night and see a little key in the back of your neck, like that *Dr Who* episode with the creepy dolls?'

His eyebrows lifted. 'Creepy dolls?'

'Haven't you ever watched that television programme?'

'I don't watch television.'

She let out a laugh. 'You really are a robot.'

'Ah, you've discovered my one deep secret. And here I thought I hid it so well.'

She laughed again, and his answering smile made everything in her lighten and lift. They'd never, ever joked around before. Teased each other. *Enjoyed* each other. It was as heady as a drug, his smile, his light tone. She craved more, and she knew just how dangerous and foolhardy that was.

Leo had made it abundantly clear last night. *As long as it's enough for you.*

Already she knew it wasn't.

'All right, then,' she said, taking a pastry from her plate. 'No secret fears, funny dreams, or embarrassing moments. How about hobbies, then?'

'Hobbies?' he repeated in something so close to incredulity that Alyse nearly laughed.

'Yes, you have heard of them? Pleasant pastimes such as reading, gardening, stamp-collecting?' He simply stared and she supplied helpfully, 'Tennis? Golf? Pottery?'

'Pottery? I thought macramé was bad enough.'

'You must do something to unwind.'

He arched an eyebrow. 'Do I seem unwound to you?'

'Now that you mention it…maybe I should suggest something? Watercolours, perhaps?'

His lips twitched and he shook his head. 'I play chess.'

'Chess?' She smiled, felt the sweet thrill of a small victory. 'I should have been able to guess that.'

'Oh? How so?'

'Chess is a game requiring patience and precision. You have both in spades.'

'I'm not sure that was a compliment,' he answered. 'But I'll take it as one.'

'Are you very good?'

'Passable.'

Which probably meant he was amazing. She could picture him in front of a chessboard, his long, tapered fingers caressing the smooth ivory shape of the queen... A shaft of desire blazed through her. She really needed to get a grip if she was fantasising about *chess*. Well, really, about Leo.

'Do you play?' he asked.

'I'm passable, but probably not as passable as you.'

'I didn't know there were degrees of passable.'

'There is when I feel your "passable" is a gross understatement.'

'We'll have to have a match.'

'You'll trounce me, I'm sure.' Yet the thought of playing chess—really, of doing anything with him—made her spirits lift. *See?* she wanted to say. *We are friends. This is working.*

But she still wanted more.

'So.' Leo pushed his plate away and nodded to hers. 'Are you finished? I'll just speak to the staff about arranging the snorkelling.'

Alyse watched him stride away as she sipped the last of her coffee. Despite her fledgling hope, she still wished that they were a normal couple. That this was a normal honeymoon. That Leo was striding away with a spring in his step instead of a man resigned to a lifetime of duty. That they'd spent last night wrapped in each other's arms, lost in mutual pleasure, instead of lying next to each other as rigid as two cadavers in a mortuary.

She could go on and on, Alyse knew, pointlessly wishing things had been different before, were different now. She forced herself to stop. *This* was what she had to deal with, to accept and make work. And this morning had been a beginning, a hopeful one. She needed to focus on that and let it be enough, for now at least. Maybe for ever.

Half an hour later they'd changed into swimsuits underneath tee-shirts and shorts and Leo was leading the way along the beach to where a gorgeous catamaran was pulled up on the sand.

Alyse came to a stop in front of the boat. 'Are we going in that?'

'I arranged it with the staff. I thought we'd have a better time if we could go out a bit farther.' He glanced at her, his brows knitted together in a frown. 'Are you all right with boats? I know some people are afraid of open water.'

His thoughtfulness touched her, belated as it was. It really was so confoundedly easy for Leo to affect her, she thought. To make her love him. 'It's fine,' she told him. 'It's great, actually. I love sailing.'

And as Leo navigated the boat out into the sea, the sun bathing them both in warm, golden light, Alyse stretched out on the bridge deck, it *was* great. It was fantastic.

She tilted her head back so the sun bathed her face and felt herself begin to relax, the tension dropping from her shoulders, her body loosening and leaning into the sun. She'd been strung as taut as a bow for far too long; it felt good to unbend.

When they were out on the open water, the sea

shimmering in every direction, Leo came and joined her on the bridge deck.

'You look like you're enjoying yourself.'

She lowered her head to smile at him, one hand shading her eyes from the dazzling sun. 'I am. It's good to be away from it all.'

He sat beside her, his long, muscular legs stretched out next to hers, his hands braced behind him. 'The media attention was a bit wild these last few months.'

'I'll say. The journalists were going through my rubbish, and my parents' rubbish, and my friends' as well.'

His mouth twisted in a grimace. 'I'm sorry.'

She shrugged in response. 'I signed up for it, didn't I? When I agreed.'

'That still doesn't make it pleasant.'

'No, but you've been living with it for your whole life, haven't you?'

His eyes narrowed, although whether just from the sun or because of what she'd said Alyse didn't know.

'I have,' he agreed without expression and then he rose from the deck. 'We're out far enough now. We can anchor soon.'

She watched him at the sails of the catamaran, the muscles of his back rippling under the tee-shirt that the wind blew taut against his body. She felt a rush of desire but also a swell of sympathy. She hadn't considered Leo's childhood all that deeply before; she knew as prince and heir he'd lived in the spotlight for most of his life.

Of course, the glare of that spotlight had intensified with their engagement. Did he resent that? Did he resent *her*, for making something he must not like worse? It was a possibility she'd never considered before, and an unwelcome one at that.

A few minutes later Leo set anchor and the catamaran bobbed amid the waves as he tossed their snorkelling equipment on the deck.

He tugged off his tee-shirt and shorts and Alyse did the same, conscious once again of the skimpiness of the string bikini she wore. She hadn't found a single modest swimming costume in her suitcases.

She looked up and there could be no mistaking the blaze of heat in his eyes. 'Your swimming costumes,' he remarked, 'are practically indecent.'

Alyse felt a prickly blush spread not just over

her face but her whole body. 'Sorry. I didn't choose them.'

'No need to apologise. I quite like them.' He handed her a pair of fins and then tugged his own on. 'What do you mean, you didn't choose them?'

'All my clothes are chosen by stylists.'

He frowned. 'Don't you see them first? And get to approve them?'

Alyse shrugged. 'I suppose I could have insisted, but...' She trailed off, not wanting to admit how cowed she'd been by Queen Sophia's army of stylists and staff who had seemed to know so much more than her, and had obviously not cared about what she thought.

At eighteen, overawed and more than a little intimidated, she hadn't possessed the courage to disagree with any of them, or so much as offer her own opinion. As the years had passed, bucking the trend had just become harder, not easier.

'I didn't realise you had so little say in such matters. I suppose my mother can be quite intimidating.'

'That's a bit of an understatement,' she answered lightly, but Leo just frowned.

'You were so young when we became engaged.'

She felt herself tense uneasily, unsure what he was implying. 'Eighteen, as you know.'

'Young. And sheltered.' His frown deepened and he shook his head. 'I remember how it was, Alyse. I know my parents can be very…persuasive. And, as the media attention grew, it might have seemed like you were caught in a whirlwind you couldn't control.'

'It did feel like that sometimes,' she allowed. 'At times it was utterly overwhelming. But I knew what I was doing, Leo.' *More or less.* 'I might have only been eighteen, but I knew my own mind.' *And her own heart.* Not that she would ever tell him that. After Leo's revelations about how he didn't even believe in love, never mind actually having ever felt it, Alyse had no intention of baring her heart. Not now, and perhaps not ever.

She forced the thought away. *This is a beginning.*

'Still…' he began, and she thought how easy it would be, to let him believe she'd been railroaded into this marriage. And there was some truth in it, after all. The media attention *had* been out of control, and in those dark moments when she'd considered breaking their engagement she'd known she didn't possess the strength to go against everything and everyone—the monarchy, the media, the adoring public. It had simply been too much.

But it wasn't the whole truth and, while it might satisfy Leo as to why she'd agreed in the first place—a question she hadn't been willing to answer last night—she wouldn't perpetuate another lie.

But neither will you tell him the real reason— that you were in love with him, and still are.

With determined flippancy she adjusted her mask and put her hands on her hips. 'How do I look? I don't think anyone can be taken seriously in flippers.'

His expression lightened into a smile, and Alyse felt a rush of relief. Now she was the one avoiding conversation. Honesty.

'Probably not,' he agreed and held out one of his own flippered feet. 'But they do the job. Are you ready?'

She nodded and a moment later they were slipping over the side of the boat. When Leo put his hands on her bared waist to steady her as she slid

into the water, Alyse felt her heart rate rocket.
Just the touch of his hands on her flesh sent an
ache of longing through her. She wanted to turn
to him, to rip off their masks and stupid fins
and forget anything but this need that had been
building in her for so long, the need she longed
to be sated. She wanted to be his lover as well
as his friend.

Then he let go of her and with a splash she
landed and kicked away from the boat, Leo
swimming next to her.

As soon as she put her face in the sea the world
seemed to open up, the ocean floor with its twists
and curves of coral stretching away endlessly in
every direction. Fish of every colour and size
darted among the coral: schools of black-and-
yellow-striped fish, one large blue fish swimming on its own and a fish that even seemed to
change colours as it moved.

Overwhelmed after just a few minutes, Alyse
lifted her head from the water. Leo immediately
did the same, taking his mask off to gaze at her
in concern. 'Are you OK?'

'Amazed,' she admitted. 'I've never seen so
many fish before. They're all so beautiful.'

'The snorkelling here is supposed to be the best in the Caribbean.'

She couldn't resist teasing him. 'You sound like a tourist advert.'

'I just do my research. You want to keep going?'

'Of course.'

They snorkelled side by side for over an hour, pointing different fish out to one another, kicking in synchronicity. At one point Leo reached for her hand and pulled her after him to view an octopus nestling in a cave of coral and they grinned at each other at the sight, Leo's eyes glinting behind his mask.

Finally, hungry and tired, they returned to the boat, hauling themselves dripping onto the deck.

'I had the staff pack us a lunch,' Leo informed her. 'They should have left it on the boat.'

Alyse sat drying in the sun while Leo took a wicker basket from one of the storage compartments and began to unpack its contents.

'Champagne and strawberries?' She surveyed the contents of the basket with her eyebrows raised. 'Quite the romantic feast.'

'Did you really expect anything else?'

She watched as he laid it all out on a blanket.

'Do you ever get tired of it?' she asked quietly. 'The pretending? With me?'

His fingers stilled around the neck of the champagne bottle and then he quickly and expertly popped the cork. 'Of course, just as I imagine you do.'

'Why did you agree to it all, Leo? Was it really just to help stabilise the monarchy?'

The glance he gave her was dark and fathomless. 'Does that not seem like enough reason to you?'

'It seems like a huge sacrifice.'

'No more than you were willing to make.'

They were getting into dangerous territory, Alyse knew. She didn't want him to ask her again why she'd agreed. She didn't want to have to answer.

'Does the monarchy matter that much to you?'

'Of course it does. It's everything to me.'

Everything. That was rather all-encompassing; it didn't leave room for much else. 'I suppose you've been preparing to be king since you were born.'

Leo didn't answer for a moment and Alyse felt the tension in his suddenly stilled hands, his long, lean fingers wrapped around the neck of the champagne bottle. Then he began to pour, the bubbles fizzing and popping against the sides of the flute. 'More or less.'

Alyse surveyed him, felt instinctively he wasn't saying something, something important. Perhaps he did have secrets…just as she did.

'Another toast?' she asked as Leo handed her a glass.

'We've had quite a few toasts recently.'

'And quite a lot of champagne.'

'People can be amazingly unoriginal about what they think is romantic,' he said dryly. He eyed her thoughtfully over the rim of his glass. 'How about a toast to friendship?'

Alyse's heart lurched. 'You're coming around, then?' she said lightly, and he inclined his head in acknowledgement.

'A bit.'

'To friendship, then,' she answered, and they both drank, their eyes meeting over the rims of their glasses. Alyse felt her insides tighten and then turn over at the look of heat in Leo's navy eyes. They simmered with it, that warmth seeming to reach out and steal right through her. For such a coldly practical man, his eyes burned. *She* burned.

'So,' she offered shakily. 'What is there to eat besides strawberries?'

'Oh, lots of things,' he said lightly, glancing away from her to fill a plate with various delectable offerings. 'You won't go hungry.'

'No,' Alyse murmured. But she *was* going hungry...hungry in an entirely different, and carnal, way. She knew he wanted her, had thrilled to the taste and feel of his desire when he'd kissed her, when he'd pulled her close to that hard, hard body. Yet she still didn't quite have the confidence to act on it now, to thrust away the plate he'd given her and reach for something far more delicious: *him.*

'Try some,' Leo offered, and she saw the heat flare in his eyes, wondered if he knew the nature of her thoughts.

Wordlessly Alyse put something in her mouth; she didn't even look to see what it was. The burst of sweet flavour on her tongue surprised her and she realised she'd bitten into a plantain fried in orange juice.

'Good?' Leo asked, and now she heard the desire in his voice as well as saw it in his eyes; it poured over her like chocolate, rich and sweet. She'd never heard him sound like this before, never felt so much in herself—or from him.

Somehow she managed to eat most of what was on her plate, the rich flavours bursting on her tongue. Every heavy-lidded look and small, knowing smile from Leo made her more aware of everything: the taste of the food; the feel of the sun on her salt-slicked skin; the heat and desire coursing through her body like warmed honey.

Finally there were only the strawberries left, and the champagne.

'And this is the only way to eat these,' Leo said, dipping a strawberry in his flute of champagne and then raising it to Alyse's parted lips.

Her heart rate skittered and her breathing hitched as she opened her mouth and took a bite of the champagne-sodden fruit. The taste on her tongue was both tart and sweet, but far headier than any champagne she could drink was the look of unabashed hunger in Leo's eyes—and the answering surge she felt in herself.

Strawberry juice dribbled down her chin and Leo's expression flared hotter as he caught it with the tip of his thumb then licked the juice from his own hand.

Alyse let out an audible shudder. Then, filled with a new daring fuelled by this heady desire, she reached for a strawberry and dunked it into her own glass of champagne. Leo's narrowed gaze followed her movements and after a heart-beat's hesitation he opened his mouth.

Her fingers near to trembling, Alyse put the strawberry to his lips. Juice ran over her fingers as he bit down, his gaze hot and hard on hers. She shuddered again, her whole body singing with awareness and need. Then Leo turned his head so his lips brushed her fingers and with his tongue he caught a drip of juice from the sensitive skin of her wrist.

Alyse let out a shocked gasp at the exquisite sensation. *'Leo...'*

And then he was pushing aside the remnants of their picnic, champagne spilling and strawberries scattering, and was reaching for her, finally, *finally* reaching for her.

His hands came hard onto her shoulders and then his mouth was hard on hers, tasting both tart and sweet from the champagne and the fruit.

His tongue swept into her mouth, tasting, searching, and then finding. Pleasure burst inside her like fireworks, like sparks of the sun, heating her all over. Alyse brought her hands up to his shoulders, her palms smoothing and then clutching the hot, bared skin.

Leo's mouth moved from her lips to her jaw and then her neck, his hand cupping her breast with only the thin, damp fabric of her bikini top between the heat of his palm and her sensitive skin.

Alyse moaned aloud, the sound escaping from her, impossible to contain, and Leo drew back.

'I'm sorry,' he murmured, smoothing her hair away from her face. 'I'm rushing like a randy schoolboy and you deserve better than that.'

She blinked, still dazed by the sensations coursing through her. Leo smiled, no more than a quirk of his mouth. 'I don't want your first time to be some hasty grope on the deck of a boat. I do have that much sensitivity, Alyse.'

Alyse blinked again, his words trickling through her, leaving ice in their wake. Her first time. Hers—not *theirs*.

Leo, she realised, thought she was a virgin.

CHAPTER SEVEN

LEO SAW THE emotions flash across Alyse's face like changes in the weather, sunshine and shadows. Even more so he felt the change in her, the tensing, the slight withdrawal even though she hadn't actually moved.

'What is it?' he asked quietly. 'What's wrong?'

She gave a little shake of her head. 'Nothing.'

He didn't believe that for a moment. Gently but firmly he took her chin in his hand, forced her to look at him. 'It's not nothing.'

Her clear grey eyes met his for a moment before she let her gaze slide away. 'Nothing to talk about now,' she said, with a not-quite-there smile.

If she was trying to sound light, she'd failed. Leo let go of her chin and sat back braced on his hands to survey her thoughtfully. She still wasn't looking at him and a tendril of hair, curly from the sea air, fell against the soft paleness of her cheek.

'Are you nervous about what will happen between us?'

She looked at him then, a small spark of humour lighting her eyes. 'You sound like something out of a melodrama, Leo. You're usually more blunt than that.'

He felt his mouth curving in an answering smile. 'I'm happy to be blunt. I want you, Alyse.' He gazed at her frankly, letting the desire that still coursed unsated through his body reveal itself in his face. 'I want you very badly. I want to touch you, to kiss you, to be inside you. And I don't want to wait very long.'

He saw an answering flare of heat in her eyes, turning them to molten silver, but her lips twisted and trembled and she looked away again. *What was going on?* 'That's admirably blunt.'

'I'll be even blunter—I think you want me just as much as I want you.' Gently he tucked that curly tendril of hair behind her ear, unable to keep his fingers from lingering on the softness of her skin. He felt her tremble in response. 'Do you deny it?'

'No,' she whispered, but she wouldn't look at him.

Frustration bit into him. *What was going on?*

Compelled to make her look at him, make her acknowledge the strength of the desire between them, he touched her chin and turned her to face him. She met his gaze reluctantly but unflinchingly, her eyes like two wide, grey pools Leo thought he could drown in. Lose himself completely.

'I want to make love to you,' he said quietly, each word brought up from a deep well of desire and even emotion inside him. 'But not here, on a hard deck. We have a lovely big bed on a lovely private beach and I quite like the idea of making love to you there.'

Her eyes widened even more, surprise flickering in their depths, and with a jolt he realised what he'd said. Confessed.

Making love. It was a term he'd never used, didn't even like. If love didn't exist beyond a simple hormonal fluctuation, then you couldn't make it. And sex, in his experience, had nothing to do with love. It wouldn't, even with Alyse.

Yet the words had slipped out and he knew that Alyse had noticed. What did she think was happening between them? What *was* happening between them?

Panic, icy and overwhelming, swamped him. Why the hell had he said that? Felt it? This was what happened when you let someone in just a little bit. Friendship be damned.

He dropped his fingers from her chin and rose abruptly from the deck, thankfully shattering the moment that had stretched between them. There would be no putting it together again; he'd make sure of that. 'We should head back,' he said tersely. 'In any case.'

He set sail, his back to her, and wondered just how he could get their relationship—he didn't even like calling it that—back on the impersonal and unthreatening footing he craved. Whatever it took, he vowed grimly, he would do it. He'd had enough of this *friendship*.

Alyse sat on the bridge deck and watched as Leo set sail for their private cove. His shoulders were now rigid with tension, every muscle taut, and she didn't know if it was because of her emotional withdrawal or his. She'd seen the flare of panic in his eyes when he'd said those two revealing words: making love.

But there would be no love in their physical

union, just immense, intense attraction. So why had he said it? Had he meant it simply as a turn of phrase that had alarmed him when he'd heard it aloud? Or, for a moment, had he actually felt something more? That alarmed him more than any mere words ever could.

Was she ridiculous to think that little slip might signify something? She knew she had a tendency to read far too much into a smile or a look. She didn't want to make the same mistake now, yet she couldn't keep herself from wondering. From hoping.

And yet, she felt her own flare of panic. What would Leo think—and feel—when she told him, as she must do, that she wasn't a virgin?

Alyse turned to face the sea, hugging her knees to her chest even though the wind was sultry. The coldness she felt came from inside, from the knowledge she'd been hiding from for too long already.

She'd blanked out that one fumbling evening that constituted all of her sexual experience, had consigned it to a terrible, heart-rending mistake and tried to pretend it hadn't happened.

But princesses—future queens—were meant

to be pure, unblemished, and she clearly was not. In this day and age, did it really matter?

It would matter, she supposed, to someone like Queen Sophia who, despite having been born into merely an upper-class family, held fast to the archaic bastions of the monarchy as if she were descended from a millennia's worth of royalty. It probably mattered to King Alessandro as well, but she didn't care about either of them. She cared about Leo.

Would it matter to him? Would he be disappointed that he wasn't her first? She had no illusions that *he* was a virgin; he surely hadn't been celibate for the six long years of their engagement, even if he'd been admirably discreet.

Anxiety danced in her belly. Worry gnawed at her mind. She didn't want to give him any reason to withdraw emotionally from her, to feel disappointed or perhaps even angry, yet she knew she would have to tell him…before tonight.

They didn't speak until the catamaran was pulled up on the beach and they were back in their private cove, and then only to talk about when they would have dinner. It was late afternoon, the sun already starting its mellow descent towards the horizon.

Alyse went to shower in the separate bathroom facilities, all sunken marble and gold taps kept in a rocky enclosure that was meant to look like a natural part of the cove.

She washed away the remnants of sea salt and sun cream and wondered what the next few hours would hold. Something had started to grow between her and Leo, perhaps even to blossom. Friendship—and perhaps something more, until he'd had that moment of panic.

Could they recapture both the camaraderie and passion they'd felt this afternoon?

What if her admission ruined it all?

It doesn't matter, she told herself. *It shouldn't matter. He might be a prince, but Leo's still a modern man...*

Even so, she felt the pinpricks of uncertainty. Of fear.

The staff were setting up another romantic dinner on the beach when Leo came out of the shower, his hair damp and curling slightly by his neck, the sky-blue of his shirt bringing out the blue in his eyes. Alyse had chosen another dress from her stylist-selected wardrobe, this one made of lavender silk, the colour like the last vestiges of sunset. It dipped daringly low in the front and then nipped in at the waist before flaring out around her legs. She left her hair down and her feet bare and went without make-up. It seemed ridiculous to bother with eyeliner or lipstick when they were on a secluded beach and the sea wind and salt air would mess them both up anyway.

Leo seemed to agree, for he took in her appearance with no more than a slight nod, yet she still felt the strength of his response, the leashed desire.

And something else. Something she didn't like—a coolness in his expression, a reserve in his manner. He didn't speak as he took her hand and led her to the table set up on the sand.

Still she was achingly aware of him, more now than ever before: the subtle, spicy scent of his aftershave; the dry warmth of his palm as he took her hand; the latent strength of his stride as she fell into step next to him.

'What shall we do tomorrow?' she asked brightly when they'd sat down and begun their starters, slices of succulent melon fanned out with paper-thin carpaccio. She was determined not to lose any ground, not to let him retreat back into his usual silence, as much as he might seem to want to. 'Go for a hike?'

Leo's mouth tightened and he speared a slice of melon. 'I need to work tomorrow.'

'Work?' Disappointment crashed over her but with effort she kept her smile in place, her voice light. 'This is your honeymoon, Leo.'

He pinned her with a steely gaze. 'I have duties, Alyse.'

'And what will the staff think of you ignoring your bride on the second full day of our holiday?' she asked, unable to keep herself from it even though she didn't want to bring up the whole pretence of their relationship. She wanted to talk about how it was becoming more real. Or it had seemed to be, this afternoon.

'I'm sure they'll understand. Being in love doesn't mean we live in each other's pockets. The last six years have proved that. We spent most of the time apart and yet no one seemed to have any trouble believing we were wildly, passionately in love.'

That wasn't quite true, Alyse knew. When the

media hadn't been celebrating their grand romance, it had been trying to create division: publishing incriminating-looking photos, composing pages and pages of speculation that she'd feared contained more than a grain of truth.

Leo looking for love with Duke's daughter Liana?

The memory still hurt.

'I realise that,' she told him when she trusted herself to speak as evenly as he had. 'But this is our honeymoon.'

'And you know just what kind of honeymoon it is.'

'What is that supposed to mean?'

'We're pretending,' he clarified, his voice cool. 'We always will be.'

'I haven't forgotten.' Alyse stared at him. His face was as blank as it ever had been, all traces of humour and happiness completely gone.

Today had been so sweet, so wonderful and so full of hope. She hated that they'd lost so much ground so quickly.

And why? Just because of that moment on the boat, when Leo had mentioned the dreaded L-word?

Was he actually spooked? *Afraid?*

The thought seemed ridiculous; Leo was always so confident, so assured. And yet Alyse couldn't think of another reason for his sudden and utter withdrawal.

The friendship—the intimacy—that had been growing between them had him scared.

The thought almost restored her hope. Scared was better than indifferent. Still, she knew there was no point pressing the issue now. That didn't mean she was going to let him off the hook quite so easily.

'I suppose I can entertain myself easily enough for a day,' she said lightly, and saw the flicker of surprise ripple across Leo's features that she was capitulating so easily. 'What work do you have to do?' she continued, and the surprise on his face intensified into discomfort. Alyse almost smiled. 'Are you working on that proposal for broadband?'

'Some paperwork,' he answered after a pause, his voice gruff, but Alyse was determined not to let the conversation sputter out. He would let her in, one way or another. Even if he was scared.

'Will you put the proposal before the Cabinet?

That's how it works, isn't it? A constitutional monarchy.'

'Yes. I hope to put it before them eventually. It's not one of my father's priorities.'

'Why not?'

Leo shrugged. 'My father has always been more interested in enjoying the benefits of being king rather than fulfilling his royal responsibilities.'

'But you're different.'

A light blazed briefly in his eyes. 'I hope so.'

'I think you are.' She spoke softly, and was gratified to see something like surprised pleasure lift the corners of Leo's mouth before he glanced away.

'I hope I can match you as queen.' She meant to sound light but the words came out in a rush of sincerity. 'I want to be a credit to you, Leo.'

'You already are. The fact that the public fell in love with you six years ago has been a huge boon to our country. You of all people must know the power of that photograph.'

She nodded slowly. 'Yes, but more than that. I want to do something more than just smile and shake hands.'

'Understandably, but don't sell a smile and a handshake short. It's more than my parents ever did.'

'Is it?'

'One of the reasons they were so keen for our engagement to go ahead is because they'd damaged the monarchy nearly beyond repair,' Leo said flatly. He speared a slice of beef with a little more vigour than necessary.

'How?'

He shrugged. 'Very public affairs, careless spending, a complete indifference to their people. It's hard to say which aspect of their lives was the most damaging.'

And he'd grown up in that environment. 'It doesn't sound like a very happy place to have your childhood,' she said quietly.

'I didn't. I went to boarding school when I was six.'

'Six?'

'I didn't mind.' A waiter had materialised on the edge of the beach and with a flick of his fingers Leo indicated for him to come forward. Alyse had a feeling he'd had enough of personal conversation, but at least he'd shared something. More than he ever had before.

Leo hadn't meant to say so much. Reveal so much. How did she do it? he wondered. How did she sneak beneath the defences he'd erected as a boy, had had firmly in place for so long? He never talked about his parents, or himself, or anything. He'd always preferred it that way and yet in these unguarded moments he discovered he almost enjoyed the conversation. The sharing.

So much for getting this relationship back on the footing he'd wanted: impersonal. Unthreatening.

Frustration blazed through him. No more *friendship*. No more conversation. There was only one thing he wanted from Alyse, and he would have it. Tonight.

Over the next few courses of their meal she made a few attempts at conversation and Leo answered politely enough without encouraging further talk. Still, she tried, and he had to admire her determination.

She wouldn't give up. Well, neither would he.

The moon had risen in the sky, sending its silver rays sliding over the placid surface of the sea. The waiter brought them both tiny glasses of liqueurs and a plate of petit fours and then left them alone, retreating silently back to the main resort.

All around them the night seemed very quiet, very still, the only sound the gentle lap of the waves against the sand. In the moonlit darkness, Alyse looked almost ethereal, her hair floating softly about her shoulders, her silvery eyes soft— yes, eyes could be soft, and thoughtful.

Desire tightened inside him and he took a sip of the sweet liqueur, felt its fire join the blaze already ignited in his belly. He wanted her, just as he'd told her that afternoon, and he would have her tonight.

And it wouldn't be making love.

They sat in silence for a few more moments, sipping their liqueurs, when Leo decided he'd had enough. He placed his glass on the table with deliberate precision. 'It's getting late,' he said, and Alyse's gaze widened before she swallowed audibly. Leo smiled and stood, stretching one hand out to her.

She rose and took it, her fingers slender and

feeling fragile in his as he drew her from the table and across the sand to their sleeping quarters.

While they'd been eating some of the staff had prepared their hut for the night. The sheets had been turned down and candles lit on either side of the bed, the dancing flames sending flickering shadows across the polished wooden floor.

The perfect setting for romance, for *love*, but Leo pushed that thought away. He stood in front of the bed and turned her to face him; her bare shoulders were soft and warm beneath his hands.

She shivered and he couldn't tell if it was from desire or nervousness. Perhaps both. He knew he needed to go slowly, even though the hunger inside him howled for satiation and release.

He slid his hands up from her shoulders to cup her face, his thumbs tracing the line of her jaw, her skin like silk beneath his fingers. 'Don't be nervous,' he said softly, for now that they were in the moment he still wanted to reassure her, even if he didn't want to engage his emotions.

'I'm not,' she answered, but her voice choked and she looked away.

In answer he brushed a feathery kiss across her jaw before settling his mouth on hers, his tongue tracing the seam of her lips, gently urging her to part for him.

And she did, her mouth yielding to his, her arms coming around him as he drew her pliant softness against him, loving the way her body curved and melted into his.

He kissed her deeply, sliding his hands from her face to her shoulders and then her hips, drawing her close to him, fitting her against the already hard press of his arousal. Desire shot up through him with fiery arrows of sizzling sensation and he felt her shudder in response.

Gently, slowly, he drew the thin straps of her dress down her shoulders. Alyse stood still, her gaze fastened on him as he reached behind her, and with one sensuous tug had her dress unzipped. It slithered down her body and pooled on the floor, leaving her in only a skimpy white lace bra and matching pants—honeymoon underwear, barely serving their purpose, unless it was to inflame—which it did.

Leo let his gaze travel slowly across her barely clothed body, revelling in the beauty of her, desire coiling tighter and tighter inside him.

He placed one hand on her shoulder, sliding it

down to her elbow, smoothing her skin. She drew a shuddering breath.

'Are you cold?'

'No.' She shook her head and, needing to touch her more—everywhere—he slid his hand from her elbow to her breast, his palm cupping its slight fullness as he drew his thumb across the aching peak. Alyse let out a little gasp and he smiled, felt the primal triumph of making her respond.

'I know this is new for you,' he said quietly and he saw a flash of something almost like anguish in her eyes.

'Leo...' She didn't say anything more and he didn't want to waste time or energy on words. Smiling, he brushed a kiss across her forehead and then across her mouth before he unhooked her bra and slid it off her arms. He drew her to him, her bare breasts brushing the crisp cotton of his shirt, and even that sensation made him ache. He wanted her so very much.

'What about your clothes?' she asked shakily and he arched an eyebrow.

'What about mine?'

'They're on you, for starters.'

He laughed softly. 'I suppose you could do something about that.'

Her fingers shook only a little as she fumbled with the buttons of his shirt, the tips of her fingers brushing his bare chest. He stood still, everything in him dark and hot from just those tiny touches. Then she finished unbuttoning it and pulled it off his shoulders, her gaze hungry as she let it rove over him, making him darker and hotter still.

His breathing hitched as she smoothed her hands over his chest, down to his abdomen, and then with a little, mischievous smile her fingers slipped under the waistband of his trousers.

He sucked in a hard breath as with her other hand she tugged on the zip, her fingers skimming the hard length of his erection. 'Alyse...'

'Only fair,' she whispered with a trembling laugh, and Leo's voice lowered to a growl as he answered,

'I'll show you fair.'

He pulled her even closer to him so her breasts were crushed against his bare chest and kissed her with a savage passion he hadn't even known he possessed, the self-control he'd prided himself on for so long slipping away, lost in a red tide of desire.

And she responded, her arms coming up around him, her tongue tangling with his as she matched him kiss for kiss, their breathing coming in ragged gasps as the shy gentleness of their undressing turned into something raw and powerful and almost harsh in its intensity.

He'd never felt like this before. Felt so much before. He wanted and needed her too much to be alarmed or afraid by the power of her feelings—or his own.

Alyse's mind was dazed with desire as Leo drew her to the bed. Ever since he'd led her from the dinner table she'd tried to find a way to tell him the truth, that she wasn't a virgin. His obvious assumption made the need for disclosure all the more vital, yet somehow the words wouldn't come. And when Leo had kissed her, and undressed her, and touched her...

Then she'd had no words at all.

She didn't remember how they ended up lying on the bed, Leo sliding off her underwear and then his own so they were both completely naked.

It had all happened so quickly, yet she felt as if she'd been waiting for this moment for ever.

And still she hadn't told him. *Maybe later*, she thought hazily as Leo bent his head to her breast and she raked his shoulders with her nails, her body arching off the bed as he flicked his tongue against her heated, over-sensitised skin. *After.* She'd tell him after.

She felt Leo's hand between her thighs, his fingers sliding deftly to the damp warmth between them and her hips arched instinctively as he found her centre.

'You're lovely,' he murmured as he touched her, brushing kisses across her mouth, her jaw, her throat. 'So lovely.'

'You are too,' Alyse answered, her voice uneven, and he laughed softly.

He slid a finger inside her and she felt her muscles instinctively clench around him. A wave of pleasure crashed over and drowned out any possible attempts at speech or thought. Leo's touch was so knowing, so assured, and her fingernails dug into the bunched muscles of his shoulders as he rolled over her, his clever fingers replaced by the hard press of his erection.

Alyse arched her hips, welcoming this glorious invasion, the sense of completeness she ached to feel with every fibre of her being.

'This might hurt just a little,' he whispered and she closed her eyes against a sudden, soul-quenching rush of shame.

She couldn't lie to him, not even by her silence. Not now, not about this.

'It won't, Leo,' she choked, her anguish all too apparent to both of them. 'I'm—I'm not a virgin.'

She felt him poised above her, could feel the heat and strength of him so close to her; another inch or two and he'd be inside her, as she so desperately wanted. She arched her hips reflexively, but he didn't move.

Alyse let out a shudder of both longing and despair. Clearly she picked her moments well.

Leo swore under his breath and eased back. 'What a time to tell me,' he said, his voice coming out in a groan.

'I didn't—didn't know how to tell you,' she whispered miserably.

Leo rolled onto his back and stared up at the woven-grass roof of the hut, his chest heaving with the effort of stopping at such a critical moment.

'Obviously it's a distressing memory,' he said after a moment, his eyes still on the roof. 'You must have been very young.'

'It was.' She took a breath, hating that they were talking about this now, in such an intimate moment, a moment that had seconds ago promised tenderness and pleasure and perhaps even the first fragile shoots of a deeper and more sacred emotion. 'And I wasn't that young. I was twenty.'

She felt Leo still next to her, every muscle in his body seeming to go rigid. Then he turned his head to stare at her, and everything in Alyse quailed at the sight of the cold blankness in his eyes. *'Twenty?'*

'Yes—at university.'

'You slept with someone at university?' he repeated, sounding so disbelieving that Alyse flinched.

'Yes—do we have to talk about this?'

'I don't particularly relish the conversation myself.' In one fluid movement Leo sat up and reached for his boxers.

Alyse felt her throat thicken as disappointment and frustrated desire rushed through her. 'Leo,

I'm sorry. I suppose I should have told you earlier, but we never had any remotely intimate conversations, and frankly I just wanted to forget it ever happened. That's no excuse, I know.' He finished sliding on his boxers and just picked up his shirt. 'Are you—are you angry? That I'm not a virgin?'

He let out a bark of humourless laughter and turned to face her. He looked as cold and remote as he ever had—only worse, because she'd seen his face softened in sleep or with a smile, his eyes warm with laughter and then hot with desire. Now he was reverting once more to the icy stranger she knew, the man who made her despair. 'You think I'm angry that you're not a virgin?'

'Well—yes.'

He shook his head, the movement seeming one of both incredulity and contempt. 'That would be a bit of a double standard, since I'm not one.'

She swallowed, surprised. 'I know, but it's always been different for men, hasn't it? And the whole princess thing…'

'This has nothing to do with the *princess thing*,' Leo answered her shortly. 'And I don't believe in double standards. If I seem angry, Alyse, it's not because you've had sex before. It's because you had sex while you were engaged to me.'

And, before she could even process that statement, he had yanked on his trousers and was heading out into the night.

CHAPTER EIGHT

LEO STRODE ACROSS the beach, knowing that, just like last night, he had nowhere to go and hating it. Damn this island. Damn Alyse. Damn himself, for caring about what she'd done—and who she'd done it with.

He didn't feel merely betrayed, which was what made him so angry. He felt hurt.

Stupid, because it had happened years ago, and it wasn't as if they'd actually loved each other. So what if she'd loved someone else? Given herself to someone else? What did it really matter?

And yet it did.

He knew he was overreacting; knew he should be at most surprised, and a little annoyed, perhaps, by her infidelity during their engagement, but he shouldn't actually *care*.

Not like this. Never like this.

'Leo?'

He turned and saw her slender form framed

in the doorway of the hut, now clothed in one of those ridiculously frothy robes, the candlelight silhouetting her slight yet still lush curves, curves he remembered the feel of under his palms. Leo turned his face away.

'Please don't storm off,' she said, the desolation in her voice reaching him in far too many ways. 'Talk to me.'

Leo didn't reply. He didn't want to talk to her, didn't want to explain the feelings that churned inside him, the feelings he wasn't sure he understood—or wanted to understand—himself.

'Please, Leo.'

Wordlessly he stalked back to the hut, his back to Alyse and the all-too-tempting image she presented in her ridiculous robe. Fine. They would have it out. She could spill all the gritty details and then he would *never* let her close again. Not as a friend. Not as a lover. He'd take her body and use her popularity and their marriage would be exactly what he'd always wanted and intended it to be. Nothing more.

She stood by the bed, the candlelight silhouetting her figure so she might as well have been naked. He tried not to gaze at the dip of her waist, those high, pert breasts, the shadow between her thighs, but still his groin ached. He'd been unbearably close to burying himself so deep inside her he would have forgotten who he was. What he actually wanted.

'I know I should have said something, maybe this afternoon,' she continued, her voice low, her fingers toying with the sash of her robe. 'But I didn't want to bring it up, to ruin what was between us—'

'There was nothing between us,' Leo cut her off harshly, too harshly. His words were loud and ragged in the hushed stillness of the night. They were *emotional*, he thought furiously.

Alyse stared at him, her eyes wide. 'Please don't say that.'

'I knew this would happen,' he continued relentlessly, remorseless now. 'A single day of barely enjoying each other's company and you're building castles in the air. Friendship never would have been enough for you.'

He saw the hurt flash across her face but she lifted her chin and managed a small smile that touched him with its bravery; he didn't *want* to be touched. 'Maybe not,' she said quietly. 'And I admit, I have a tendency to build those kinds of castles. I've been doing it ever since I met you.'

He stilled, every nerve tautening with sudden apprehension, even alarm. 'What are you talking about?'

Alyse drew a shuddering breath. 'I've been in love with you since I met you, Leo. Since my eighteenth birthday party.'

She *really* didn't choose her moments well. Alyse saw the shock blaze in Leo's eyes, followed quickly by something that looked almost like fury.

She shouldn't have told him now, should *never* have told him. Yet how could she keep the secret of her feelings any longer? How could she make him understand what had driven her recklessly into another man's arms—if only for one unfortunate night—if he didn't know how much she loved him?

'You love me,' he repeated, and she heard derision.

'I do,' she answered steadily. 'I fell in love with you at my party…'

He arched an eyebrow, his mouth twisting unpleasantly. 'Did you fall in love with the way

I danced? Or perhaps the way I drank champagne?'

'I just fell in love with you,' she answered helplessly. 'I can't explain it. Trust me, I've tried to explain it to myself many times.'

'Such a conundrum,' he drawled, his contempt evident in every taut line of his face.

He didn't believe her, Alyse realised. She hadn't expected that. Surprise, perhaps, or even horror—but incredulity? She spread her hands. 'Why do you think I agreed to the engagement? To our marriage?'

'Not because you *loved* me.'

'I couldn't imagine life without you,' Alyse blurted, the words spilling out of her. 'And I knew—of course, I've always known—you didn't love me back. But I hoped, like your father had said, that love or at least affection might come with time. That's why I kept at it, at the pretending—because I *hoped*—'

'And did that hope lead you into another man's bed, Alyse?' Leo cut her off, his voice wintry. 'Because I can do without that kind of love, thank you very much.'

'It was a mistake,' she whispered. 'A terrible mistake.'

His expression only grew colder. 'Clearly.'

She swallowed, hating that she had to rake this all up, yet knowing she needed to come clean. She'd hidden this heartache and shame for too long already. Maybe confession would help her— and Leo—to move on. 'It was one night, Leo. One awful night. That's all.'

'Is that supposed to make it more excusable?'

She felt the first flicker of anger. 'For someone who doesn't believe in double standards, you're sounding like a bit of a hypocrite.'

'A hypocrite?' He raised his eyebrows. 'How do you reckon that?'

'It's not as if you've been celibate for the last six years,' she answered, and she watched his mouth form a smile that held no humour or happiness at all.

'Haven't I?' he asked softly, his words seeming to reverberate through the room, through the stillness of the night and of her own soul. *He couldn't actually mean...?*

'But—but six *years*...' she stammered, and his smile turned hard.

'Yes, I'm well aware of how long a period of time it was.'

She shook her head slowly. 'I never thought— or expected— The engagement wasn't *real*...'

'On the contrary, our engagement has always been real. So is our marriage. It's the emotion you insist you've been feeling that isn't, Alyse. You don't love me. You don't even know what love is. A schoolgirl crush? A shaft of desire?' He shook his head, the movement one of both dismissal and derision. 'That's all love ever is. And, in any case, you don't even know me. How on earth could you think you loved me?'

She shook her head again, drew in a shuddering breath. She still couldn't believe he'd been celibate for so long. For her. 'But the magazines— they said you were with Liana Aterno.'

'You believed them? You know how they stir up gossip. You've experienced it yourself.'

'I know, but I thought— I expected you'd have some discreet liaisons. The Queen—' She stopped abruptly and Leo narrowed his eyes.

'The Queen,' he repeated softly. 'What did my mother say to you?'

'Only that I shouldn't expect you to—to be faithful.'

'Only?'

Alyse gave him a watery smile. 'She did the whole "men have needs" spiel, and how I was to turn a blind eye.'

'My mother was basing her experience on my father,' Leo answered shortly. 'And their marriage, which has been nothing but unpleasant and acrimonious. I wouldn't ever listen to marriage advice from her.'

'I was only eighteen. I didn't know any better, I suppose.'

Leo nodded, his expression still cold. He hadn't softened in the least towards her, or her indiscretion, no matter what his mother might have said. 'Well, you clearly used my mother's advice as a justification for your own behaviour.'

'It wasn't like that, Leo.'

'I don't really want to hear.'

'And I don't want to tell you, but you've got to understand.' She was stumbling over her words in her haste to explain, to reach him. 'It was one awful night. A friend from university. I was drunk.'

'I really don't need these details.'

She stared at him miserably. 'I know, but I just want you to understand. I'd seen a photo of you with that duke's daughter, Liana, in a magazine. There were articles all over the place about how you were dumping me for her.'

'And you never thought to ask me about it?'

'I never asked you about anything! We never talked. I didn't even have your mobile or your email address.'

'I think,' Leo said coldly, 'you could have got in touch if you'd wanted to. In any case, it doesn't even matter.'

She blinked, stared. 'It—doesn't?'

'No. Admittedly, I'm disappointed you thought so little of the agreement we'd made, the vows we would say. I know we've been pretending to be in love, Alyse, but we weren't pretending that we were going to get married. The rings on both our fingers is a testament to that.'

'I know,' she whispered. She felt the first sting of tears and blinked hard. 'I wish it had never happened.'

'Like I said, it doesn't matter. Naturally, I expect you to be faithful to me during our marriage. What happened in the past we can forget about. Thank God the press never found out.' He turned away from her, towards the bed, and Alyse watched him miserably. She'd never felt as far away from him as she did now...and it was her own fault.

'I'm sorry,' she said quietly.

'Like I said, it's in the past. Let's go to bed.' His meaning was clear as he slid beneath the sheets, his back to her: they would not be consummating their marriage tonight.

Swallowing, Alyse slid into bed next to him. They lay there silently, the only sound the ragged draw and tear of their breathing and the whoosh of the waves on the sand. She could feel the heat of his body, inhaled the scent of his aftershave, and her body still pulsed with longing. Yet she'd never felt farther away from him, or from hope, than she did in this moment.

She knew it was her own fault. She thought of that single night four years ago and closed her eyes in shame. It had been a terrible lapse of judgement, a moment of weakness she'd tried to block out since.

She'd been revising for exams and had caught

sight of that awful photograph of Leo laughing with Liana, a gorgeous icy blonde, in a way he never had with her. Jealousy had sunk its razor-sharp claws into her soul, bled out her heart.

She'd been just twenty years old, engaged to Leo for two years, having seen him only a handful of times and spoken to him even less—yet firm, so firm, in the belief she loved him. And in that moment she'd felt certain he would never love her. Never even laugh with her.

It was the closest she'd ever come to breaking off the engagement, but even at her lowest point, halfway to heartbroken, she'd known she couldn't do it. Didn't possess the strength to call a halt to a romance that had captivated the world and still didn't want to.

Yet her despair at feeling that Leo would never love her, never even like her, had led her to go out with a casual friend—Matt—and get far too drunk on cheap cider.

Even now the details of the evening were fuzzy; they'd gone back to her flat and started talking. She'd been drunk enough to be honest, too honest, and she'd said something about how Leo didn't actually love her.

Matt had laughed and said that was impossible; everyone knew how they loved each other madly. Alyse had been just sober enough to keep from insisting on the truth, but she'd stared at that picture of Leo with the lovely Liana—she'd bought the magazine, if only to torture herself—and something in her had broken.

Without thinking about what she was doing, she'd reached for Matt and kissed him clumsily. She still didn't know what had driven that impulse, perhaps just a desperate need for someone to want her.

He had responded eagerly, both alarming and gratifying her, and somehow it had all got out of control. In her drunken state she hadn't been able or even willing to stop it.

The next morning Matt had been sheepish and she'd been stricken. She'd felt ashamed and dirty, yet also strangely defiant, imagining Leo with the lovely Liana. Hating the thought of it, and hating what she'd done too.

Just as Leo hated it. He believed her one indiscretion showed her love for the flimsy fairy tale he thought it was—and lying there, wide awake and restless, she felt the first seed of doubt burrow deep into her heart, its shell cracking apart all her certainties.

What if Leo was right?

Too restless to lie still any longer, Alyse slid from the bed and headed out to the beach. The sand was cool and soft beneath her bare feet and the sky above was inky black and spangled with stars. The air was cooler now, and in only her nightdress she felt goose bumps rise on her arms.

She sat on the sand, as miserable as she'd ever been when she'd believed herself to be hopelessly in love with Leo. And this time it was because she had a sudden, sneaking fear that she wasn't, and perhaps never had been.

What did that say about her? Could she really have been so childish, so deluded, so *wrong* to convince herself she loved a man she barely knew? And to have kept believing it for so long?

Resting her chin on her knees, Alyse thought back to that first fateful night when Leo had come to her birthday party. Her mother had been almost as excited as she was, telling her that she'd been friends with Sophia in school, and how Leo was such a handsome prince… She'd reminded her too, of course, of the way she'd fallen in love with Alyse's father Henri at a party just like that one, across a crowded room…

Just like she'd convinced herself she had with Leo.

Had she wanted her parents' fairy tale for herself? Was that why she'd convinced herself of her love for Leo, because in her loneliness and uncertainty she'd longed for something more, had half-believed she could have it with Leo?

Everyone else had seemed to think she could, and in her innocence and immaturity she'd allowed a girlish attraction to become something so much bigger and deeper in her own mind and heart. And had continued to believe it, because as time went on and the media frenzy had grown, *not* to believe it took more strength and courage than she'd ever possessed.

Alyse let out a soft groan and pressed her forehead against her drawn-up knees. She didn't want to believe she'd been so deluded, didn't want to let go of her love so easily, so awfully.

And yet the derision on Leo's face had cut her to the bone, to the soul. *You don't even know me.*

No, she didn't, although she was starting to know him now. And, despite her parents' love-at-first-sight story, she wasn't sure she could believe it for her and Leo.

But that didn't mean she couldn't love him now. Learn to love him, the real him, the man she still wanted to believe hid underneath that mask, that armour of cold purpose and ruthless efficiency. He was there; she'd seen glimpses over the years and even more in the last few days. Glimpses that had stole through her soul and touched her heart.

He was there…and farther away from her than ever.

Sighing, her body cold and aching now, Alyse rose from the sand and headed back to the hut. She didn't know what tomorrow, or any of her tomorrows, would now hold. How Leo would feel or act. How they could get back just a little bit of the camaraderie they'd shared.

And as for love?

Her mouth curved in a humourless smile. She didn't dare even think about that now.

She must have slept, although she didn't remember doing so as she'd lain next to Leo's hard body. But when she next opened her eyes sunlight was flooding the little hut and Leo was gone.

Alyse rose and dressed quickly, tossing the lavender silk dress Leo had stripped from her body into one of her cases with a wince. If only the night had ended differently and she'd woken up in Leo's arms...

'Good morning.'

She glanced up, her heart rate skittering as he came into the tent. He was showered and dressed and he looked coldly impassive, no expression at all lightening the navy of his eyes or softening those impossibly stern features. Even so all Alyse had to do was look at him to remember the way his lips had felt on hers, hard and soft at the same time, and how his hands had felt on her body... tormenting her with such exquisite pleasure.

She swallowed hard and looked away. 'Good morning.'

'Sleep well?' he queried, his voice holding a slight, mocking edge, and Alyse shook her head.

'No.'

'Pity. Breakfast is in the pavilion again. I've already eaten.'

'You have?' He'd turned away from her and she stared at his broad back, the stiff set of his shoulders. 'People will talk, you know,' she said, even though she hated using that excuse. She didn't care what people said. She cared only what Leo thought. What he felt…or didn't feel.

'I told them you were having a lie-in after a busy night, and made all the waitresses blush.'

'You didn't.'

'No, I didn't.' He turned around then, his eyes snapping with suppressed anger. 'I've developed a distaste for lying, even to the staff. But they assumed it anyway, so don't worry, our cover isn't blown.'

'Leo, I want to talk to you—'

'And I want to talk to you,' he cut her off coolly. 'But you might as well eat first.' And, reaching for the newspaper he'd brought from the pavilion, he settled in a chair and snapped it open, managing to ignore Alyse completely.

Without another word she left the hut.

Leo stared unseeingly at the newspaper in front of him, amazed at the amount of rage that poured through him in a scalding river. Why on earth was he so angry? He couldn't remember feeling this much emotion before, and it infuriated him—and frightened him. He was honest enough to admit that at least to himself.

No matter what he'd just told her, he wasn't about to admit it to Alyse.

And, when she returned from breakfast, he'd tell her exactly what he had in mind: a return to Maldinia and to their earlier arrangement, an arrangement that had satisfied him exactly. Their marriage would be a matter of business and convenience, nothing more. He'd been a fool to allow her to entertain ideas of friendship or affection. Both were pointless and had only raised ridiculous hopes in Alyse.

And in himself.

That annoyed and angered him most of all— that he'd actually enjoyed their time together, their banter, and of course their kisses… Just remembering how close he'd been to being inside her made Leo shift uncomfortably in his chair, a persistent ache in his groin.

He still wanted her, and he'd have her, perhaps even tonight. There was no longer any need to wait. He wasn't going to concern himself with her feelings, her fears. They'd return to the firm footing he had thought they'd been on when they'd both said those wretched vows.

To have and to hold, from this day forward...

Yes, from this day forward he would know exactly what to expect. And so would Alyse.

She returned to their sleeping quarters half an hour later and Leo glanced up as she approached, forcing himself not to notice the tender, bruised-looking skin under her eyes or the way her lush, pink mouth turned down at the corners. She wore a silky tee-shirt in pale green and a swishy skirt that blew around her long, slim legs. He yanked his gaze upwards, found it settling on the rounded curve of her breasts and determinedly moved it up to her face.

'Leo, I wanted to—'

'Let me tell you what I want to say,' he cut her off, his voice clipped. He had no wish to hear her stammered, desperate apologies or excuses. Neither mattered. 'This whole idea of friendship was a mistake,' he stated flatly. Alyse stilled, her face carefully blank so he couldn't tell at all what she was thinking or feeling.

Not that he cared.

'It was against my better judgement in the first

place,' he continued. 'It just complicates matters. It was much simpler and easier before.'

'When we pretended all the time?' Alyse filled in.

'We'll always be pretending,' he answered, his tone deliberately brutal. 'The public expects to see us wildly in love—and, as I've told you before, that will never happen.'

'And here I thought you'd developed a distaste for lying.'

He had. Lord, how he had. He'd been doing it his whole life, just as his parents had been doing it with him. And he'd hated it all, hated how it hurt him, yet he'd thought with Alyse it would be different. It had been his choice and he would be in control.

And so he would. Starting now.

'Sometimes needs must,' he said brusquely. 'But at least we won't lie to each other.'

'So what exactly are you proposing, Leo? That we ignore each other for the length of our honeymoon? Our marriage?'

'Our honeymoon is over,' he answered, and he watched her pale.

'Over?'

'We head back to Maldinia this morning.'

'This morning.' Alyse stared at him, her face white. Then she rallied, a spark of challenge firing her eyes so Leo felt a reluctant surge of admiration for her spirit. 'So we had a honeymoon of all of two days. How do you think the public—the press—will react to that?'

'It's up to us, isn't it? If we return to Averne with faces like a wet weekend then, yes, they might suspect something. But if we smile and present a united front—royal duty must come first, after all—then I don't think we should have a problem.' He raised his eyebrows and smiled coolly. 'I trust that after six years your acting ability is up to the challenge.'

'And what about our scheduled visits to London? Paris? Rome?'

'We can fly from Maldinia. They're not until next week.'

Alyse just shook her head. 'Why do you want to return to Maldinia?' she asked quietly.

'Because I'd like to get our marriage on its proper footing,' Leo answered, his voice coming out in something close to a snap. He strove to level it. 'And that doesn't involve romping around on the beach or playing at being friends on a boat.'

Alyse gazed at him thoughtfully and it took all of his effort not to avert his gaze, to hide from it. 'You're scared,' she finally said, and Leo let out an abrupt, incredulous laugh.

'Scared? Of what?'

'Of me—of what was happening between us. Intimacy.'

'Please.' He held up one hand. 'Spare me your fanciful notions. I had enough of them last night, when you tried to convince me you loved me.'

'I thought I loved you.'

'You've since been disabused of the notion? How convenient.' He felt a flash of hurt and suppressed it. 'I'll go tell the staff to come fetch our bags.' And without a backward glance he stalked out of the hut.

CHAPTER NINE

ALYSE SAT ON the jet across from Leo. In the seven hours since they'd left St Cristos he hadn't spoken to her once. They'd flown overnight, sleeping in separate beds, and now it was morning with the sky hard and bright around them, and cups of coffee, a platter of croissants and fresh fruit set on the coffee table between them.

Leo was scanning some papers, his expression calm and so very collected, while she felt as if she'd swallowed a stone, her insides heavy and leaden, her eyes gritty with exhaustion, both emotional and physical.

They hadn't spoken since that awful exchange in their hut, when Leo had told her they were returning to Maldinia. She had no illusions about what would happen there; in a huge palace, with all of his royal duty beckoning, he would find it entirely easy to ignore her. They would see each other only for royal functions and occasions, and live separate lives the rest of the time.

Just like their engagement.

She swallowed, a hot lump of misery lodging in her throat. She couldn't go back to that. She couldn't live like that, not in Averne, where she wouldn't even have the comfort of her studies and her own circle of friends to bolster her, the way she'd had in Durham—a little bit, at least.

She supposed, like Leo, she could focus on her royal duty. She had a service to perform as a princess of Maldinia, a duty to the country's people, and she'd enjoyed and looked forward to that aspect of her royal life. Yet the thought of making it her entire purpose depressed her beyond measure.

She wanted more.

You've always wanted more. You gambled on this engagement, this marriage, in the hope of more—and now it looks like you'll never have it.

She felt a hot rush behind her lids and blinked hard. She would *not* cry. There had to be some way to salvage this, some way to reach Leo again, to make him understand and open up to her once more. But how?

Closing her eyes, she pictured his unyielding face, the grim set of his mouth and eyes as he'd spoken to her that morning. He'd seemed colder than he ever had before, almost as if he *hated* her.

How had it all gone so disastrously wrong so quickly? They'd been making steps—baby steps, true, but still *progress:* drawing closer to each other, enjoying each other's company. And then in one terrible moment everything had splintered apart. Everything had become worse than before because, instead of being merely indifferent to her, Leo was now angry.

Emotional.

Alyse stilled, realisation and hope trickling slowly, faintly through her. Why would Leo be so angry, so emotional, unless…?

Unless he cared?

Thoughts tumbled through her mind, a kaleidoscope of emotions and hopes. Maybe he'd enjoyed their brief time together more than he wanted to admit. Perhaps he was angry because he'd been hurt—and of course he wouldn't like that. He'd hate it.

Knowing Leo—and she was knowing him more and more every day—he'd fight against feeling anything for her. She didn't understand exactly why he resisted emotion and denied love so vehemently, but she knew there had to be a deep-seated reason, something most likely to do with his family and upbringing. And, when things got sticky, difficult and painful, of course he would revert back to his cold, haughty self. His protective persona, his only armour.

So how could she slip underneath it, touch the heart hidden beneath? How could she breach his defences, crack open his shell?

Sighing, Alyse opened her eyes and stared at the man across from her, his focus still solely on the papers in front of him.

'Leo,' she said, and reluctantly he lifted his gaze from the papers, his expression chillingly remote.

'Yes?'

'Are you really going to ignore me for the rest of this flight? For our entire lives?'

His mouth tightened and his gaze swept over her in unflinching assessment. 'Not ignore, precisely,' he answered coolly. 'I don't, for example, intend to ignore you tonight.'

Shock blazed through her, white-hot. 'Are you

saying,' she asked in a low voice, 'that you intend to—to consummate our marriage tonight?'

Leo's expression didn't change at all. 'That's exactly what I'm saying.'

Alyse licked her dry lips. Even now she could not keep a tide of longing from washing over her. She still wanted him, cold and angry as he was. She would always want him. 'Even though you can barely summon the will to speak to me?' she observed and he arched an eyebrow.

'Speaking won't be involved.'

She flinched. 'Don't be crass. No matter how cold this business arrangement is, we both deserve more than that.'

An emotion—she couldn't quite tell what—flickered across his face and he glanced away. 'As long as you realise that's exactly what this is,' he answered. 'A business arrangement.'

'Trust me,' she replied. 'I'm not likely to forget.'

Nodding in apparent satisfaction, Leo returned to his papers. Alyse sank against the sumptuous sofa, closing her eyes once more. So, she thought with a swamping sense of desolation, the only thing he wanted from her now was her body.

But what if, along with her body, she gave him her heart?

She stilled, opened her eyes and gazed blindly ahead. She'd just realised herself that she'd never actually loved him; her feelings for him had been part schoolgirl infatuation, part desperately wishful thinking. So how could she now offer this cold, proud, *hurting* man her heart?

Because that's what I want for my marriage. Because even if she hadn't loved him all of these years, she knew she could love him now. She could fall in love with him if he let her, if she got to know him as she had done over the last few days.

And that could begin tonight.

Five silent hours later they had landed in Maldinia on a balmy summer morning and returned by royal motorcade to the palace, unspeaking all the while.

The reporters had managed to get word of their early arrival and were waiting both at the airport and in front of the palace. They posed for photographs in both places, smiling and waving, Leo's arm snug around her waist. She glanced at him out of the corner of her eye and saw that, despite the white flash of his smile and his seemingly relaxed pose, his body was rigid next to her, his eyes flinty. He might be willing to pretend, but he certainly wasn't enjoying it. And neither was she.

Once they were back in the palace, Leo disappeared to his study and Alyse was shown to the bedroom she would have as her own—and it was clearly her own, not hers and Leo's; it was a feminine room in pale blues and greys, gorgeous and utterly impersonal.

She sank onto the bed, feeling lonely, lost and completely miserable. A few minutes later, still lost in her own unhappy thoughts, a knock sounded on the door and, without waiting for a response, Queen Sophia swept in.

Alyse stood up, a wary surprise stealing through her. She'd had very few interactions with her haughty mother-in-law and she preferred it that way.

Now Queen Sophia arched one severely plucked eyebrow and swept a thoroughly assessing gaze over Alyse. 'Why have you returned from the honeymoon so early?'

Alyse licked her dry lips. 'Leo— He had work to do.'

'Work? On his honeymoon?' Sophia's mouth pinched tight. 'How do you think the public will react to that? They want to see a young married couple in love, you know. They want to see you celebrating. The monarchy still depends on you.'

Alyse thought of what Leo had said about his parents: their affairs, careless spending and utter indifference to their own people. In light of all that, Sophia's insistence on royal decorum seemed hypocritical at best. 'I would think,' she answered, her voice wavering only slightly, 'the monarchy depends on you just as much.'

Sophia's mouth tightened further and her pale-blue eyes flashed ice. 'Don't be impertinent.'

'I wasn't. I was being honest.'

'I can do without your honesty. The only reason you've risen so high is because we decided it would be so.'

'And the only reason you decided it would be so is because it benefitted you,' Alyse retorted, a sudden anger and courage rising up inside her. 'With Leo and I in the spotlight, you could continue to do as you pleased—which it seems is all you've ever done.' Two spots of bright colour appeared on Sophia's high cheekbones. 'Oh, I know it grates on you,' Alyse continued, her temper now truly lit. 'To see your precious first-born married to a commoner.'

'Precious first-born?' Sophia's mouth twisted. 'Has Leo not even told you about his brother? But then I suppose he doesn't tell you anything.'

Alyse stared at her, nonplussed. 'His brother…?'

'Alessandro. His older brother. My husband disinherited him when he was twenty-one and Leo was eighteen. He would have been King.' For a second, no more, Alyse thought she heard a faint note of bitterness or even sorrow in Sophia's voice. Had she loved her son Alessandro? Loved him, perhaps, more than Leo?

'We don't talk about him,' Sophia continued flatly. 'The media stopped raking his story up over and over again years ago. But, if you wondered why the monarchy needed to be stabilised and restored, why we needed *you*, it's because of the scandal of Sandro leaving the way he did.' Sophia's eyes flashed malice. 'I'm surprised Leo never told you.'

Alyse didn't answer. She didn't sound at all surprised. Had Sophia guessed her schoolgirl feelings for Leo; had she perhaps used them against her all those years ago when she'd suggested their engagement? It seemed all too possible. She was shrewd and calculating and those ice-blue eyes missed nothing.

'Be careful,' Sophia continued softly. 'If the sorry truth of your relationship with Leo comes out now, the scandal will consume us all, including you. You might have enjoyed all the attention these last few years, but it won't be quite so pleasant when everyone starts to hate you.' Sophia's mouth curved in a cruel smile. 'Besides, you'd be no use to us then. No use to Leo.'

Alyse just stared, her mind spinning sickly, and with a click of her heels Sophia was gone, the door shutting firmly behind her.

Alyse sank back onto the bed. Had the Queen's parting shot been a threat? *No use to Leo.* If the media ever turned on her, if she became a liability to the monarchy rather than an asset, would Leo still want to be married to her?

It was a horrible question to ask herself, and even worse to answer. Knowing just what he thought of their marriage, she had a terrible feeling he wouldn't.

And what about his brother? She could hardly be surprised that Leo had never told her about Alessandro; he had told her barely anything personal about himself.

And yet, it could explain so much. She'd suspected his sense of cold detachment stemmed from his upbringing; with parents like King Alessandro and Queen Sophia, how could it not?

But a brother? A brother who had perhaps been the favourite, who had gone his own way, leaving Leo to try and make up for his absence? To prove himself through his endless royal duty?

She knew she was making assumptions, trying to understand the man who still seemed so much of an enigma to her.

The man who would come to her tonight...

She felt a shiver of anticipation for what lay ahead. Was it wrong—or perhaps just shameless—of her actually to be looking forward to tonight, at least in part? No matter how little Leo felt for her now, she still wanted him. Desperately.

Alyse didn't see Leo until that evening, when the royal family assembled for a formal dinner. He looked stunning in black tie, which was the standard dress for these cold family dinners. King Alessandro and Queen Sophia preferred this kind of rigid formality, and as she sat down across from Leo she wondered how it had affected him. How it had affected his brother.

It still surprised her that she'd never even known about him, not from Leo, not from his family, not even from any of the articles she'd read about the Maldinian royal family. *Her* family.

Her and Leo's engagement, and the accompanying scrutiny and excitement, must have taken the attention away from Leo's brother, almost as if everyone had forgotten it. Him.

Everyone but Leo. Somehow she didn't think he had forgotten his brother. She wanted to ask him about it, wanted to learn more about this man and what made him the way he was, and yet…

From the cool expression on Leo's face, he didn't want to have much conversation—not with anyone, and especially not with her.

The dinner was, as Alyse had expected, stilted and mainly silent. Alessandro and Sophia both made a few pointed references to their early return from honeymoon, but Leo was indifferent to any criticism, and Alyse just murmured something about looking forward to settling into life in the palace.

As if.

Alexa shot her an encouraging look when she made that remark, her dark-blue eyes—the same colour as Leo's—flashing both spirit and sympathy. Alyse knew Alexa was engaged to marry a sheikh of a small Middle Eastern country next year, and she had a feeling her new sister-in-law didn't relish the union. At least, Alyse thought with a sigh, Alexa hadn't had to pretend to be in love with her fiancé. As far as Alyse knew, she'd only seen him a handful of times.

By ten o'clock the dinner was finished and Sophia was about to rise first to escort everyone out to the salon where they would have coffee and petits fours. It was another part of the formal ritual, and one Leo forestalled as he rose before his mother.

'It's been a very long day. Alyse and I will retire.'

Alyse felt herself blush even though there had been no innuendo in Leo's words, just a statement of fact. Sophia looked frostily affronted but

Leo didn't even wait for her acquiescence as he took Alyse by the hand and led her from the dining room.

'Your mother doesn't like her order interrupted,' Alyse murmured as they headed upstairs. Her heart was pounding hard and her head felt weirdly light.

'My mother doesn't like anyone to do anything except what she commands,' Leo answered shortly. 'She'll have to get used to disappointment.'

They'd reached the top of the stairs and he drew her down the hallway to a wood-panelled door, opening it to reveal a luxurious and very masculine bedroom. The duvet on the canopied king-sized bed had been turned down and a fire blazed in the huge stone hearth.

Alyse swallowed in a desperate attempt to ease the dryness of her throat. 'This all looks very romantic.'

'Are you being cynical?'

'No, Leo.' She turned to him, tried to smile. She wasn't going to let this evening descend into something base and soulless, or even just physical. 'I was just stating a fact. Don't worry, I don't think you had anything do with it.'

Leo gazed at Alyse, graceful, slender and so achingly beautiful. She looked both vulnerable and strong, he thought and he felt a blaze of something like admiration for her presence, her self-possession. Then he pushed that feeling away, hardened his heart—if that was indeed the organ that was being so wayward—and said coolly, 'I certainly didn't.' She stood a few feet away from him and he beckoned her forward. 'Come here.'

'Is that a command?'

'A request.'

She let out a shaky laugh. 'Rather ungraciously made, Leo.' Yet she moved towards him, head held high, her eyes flashing with spirit.

Leo made no reply, because in truth he didn't know what to say, how to act. He didn't want sex between them to be romantic. He didn't want either of them engaging their emotions. Ever.

He wanted it to be nothing more than a necessary—and, albeit physically, pleasurable—transaction, yet he was already afraid it couldn't be. Already be realised that his feelings for Alyse had changed too much for this to be simple—or sordid.

With the tiniest, trembling smile on her lips, she took another step towards him. Leo watched her hips sway under the silky fabric of her evening dress, a halter-top style in ivory that hugged every slender curve. 'Why don't you take that off?' he said, his voice already thickening with desire.

'Oh, Leo.' She let out a soft laugh. 'Why don't you take it off me?' And, despite the sorrow in that laugh, he heard a hint of a challenge in her voice and he knew she wasn't going to make this easy for either of them. 'Just because this is necessary doesn't mean we can't enjoy the experience,' she continued quietly. 'You desire me, Leo, and I desire you. That's something.'

He didn't answer, because he couldn't. Somehow his throat had thickened; his blood pounded and his fingers itched to touch her. He'd thought at first she'd make it awkward by resisting, or at least not responding to his touch—a show of defiance.

Compliance, he realised then, was far more dangerous. Still he tried to keep himself emotionally distant, if physically close, knowing how difficult a task it was that he'd set himself.

Wordlessly he reached behind her and undid the halter tie of her dress. The garment slithered off her shoulders, and with one sinuous shrug it slid from her body and pooled at her feet. She gazed at him steadily, a faint blush tingeing her cheeks pink even as she kept her head held high.

She was magnificent. He'd seen her naked before but tonight it was different; tonight it was more. She wore a strapless lacy bra and matching pants, both skimpy items highlighting the lithe perfection of her body.

'I don't think I'm the only one who's meant to be naked,' Alyse said, and he heard both a smile and a tremble in her voice. She reached for the buttons on his shirt and, mesmerised, Leo watched as she undid them, her fingers long and elegant. Her hands smoothed over the already heated skin of his chest and shoulders as she pulled the tie and then the shirt off him.

She'd undressed him last night, had unbuttoned his shirt just like this and, while it had inflamed him then, it moved him now. Touched him in ways he wasn't prepared for, didn't want.

He pushed the emotion away and reached for her, needing to obliterate his thoughts—his *feelings*—with the purely physical. And at first the taste and touch of her lips against his was enough to accomplish his goal. He plundered her mouth, slid his hands through the luxuriant softness of her hair, brought her nearly naked body in achingly exquisite contact with his. All of it was enough to stop the unwanted feeling, the impossible emotion.

Almost.

Her response undid him. She wasn't just unresisting, she was more than compliant. She answered him kiss for kiss, touch for touch, and he could feel the surrender in her supple body, the giving of herself. The offering.

With Alyse sex would never be a soulless transaction. Already it was something else, something he couldn't want and yet desperately needed. He deepened the kiss.

Alyse matched him, her body molding and melting into his, her head tilted back as she emitted a low moan from deep in her throat, the sound swallowed by his own mouth. Desire consumed him in a white-hot flame; thoughts and feelings blurred and coalesced into one.

He was barely aware of unhooking her bra, sliding off her pants; distantly he felt her hands fumble boldly at his zip and then his trousers sliding down his legs. He kicked them off in one abrupt, impatient movement and, sweeping her up in his arms, her skin silken against his, he brought her to the bed.

Even now he fought against all he was feeling. She lay back on the pillows, arms spread, thighs splayed, everything about her open and giving. She gazed up at him without embarrassment or fear; even her gaze was open to him, open and trusting. Kneeling before her, his own body naked and vulnerable, his desire on obvious and proud display, Leo felt humbled.

Humbled and ashamed that he had been attempting something he now knew was impossible: emotionless sex with Alyse. With his wife.

She held out her arms to him. 'Make love to me, Leo,' she said softly, and he let out a sound that was something between a near-sob and a laugh. How had this woman reached him—reached him and felled him—so easily? His jaded cynicism fell away and his cold, hard heart warmed and softened into pliant yielding as he came to her, enfolded her body into his and buried his face in the warm, silken curve of her neck.

In response she curled around him, arching her body into his, giving him everything she had. Leo took it as his mouth claimed hers and his hands explored her warm, supple curves; then his body found hers as he slid inside and they joined as one—one flesh, one person. It felt holy and sacred, infinitely pleasurable, and so much more than he'd ever expected or thought he wanted.

His last cold reserve broke on the sweetness of her response as he drove into her again and again, losing himself, blending into her until he didn't know where he ended and she began. And, even more amazingly and importantly, such a distinction no longer mattered.

Alyse lay back on the pillows, her whole body thrumming with pleasure. Leo had rolled onto his back next to her, one arm thrown over his face. As her heart rate began to slow from a thud she felt the perspiration cooling on her skin, the slight chill of the night air from the open windows…and the fact that she couldn't see Leo's expression. She had no idea what he was thinking or feeling at all.

Just moments ago when he'd been touching her—been *inside* her—she'd felt so close to him, in such glorious union that all of her fears and doubts had been blown away, scattered like so much cold ash.

Now they returned, settling inside her, unwelcome embers fanning into painful flame.

She'd given everything to Leo in that moment, everything she had in her to give… But perhaps even now he'd turn away from her, slide off the bed and stalk to the bathroom, as coldly indifferent as ever. Even as she braced herself for it she knew she couldn't keep herself from being hurt, or even devastated. She might not love him— yet—but she'd still given more to this man than to any other.

She felt Leo stir next to her and still she was afraid to say anything, to break whatever delicate bond held them together in this moment, the remnants of their love-making. Words would, she feared, sound like challenges to Leo, perhaps accusations or even ultimatums. For once she wanted simply to let this moment be whatever it was, and not demand or yearn for more.

Slowly he moved his arm from covering his face and swung up so he was sitting on the edge of the bed, his feet on the floor, his back to her.

'I'll get us something to drink,' he said and, slipping on his boxer shorts, he went to the *en suite* dressing room.

Alyse lay there for a moment, increasingly conscious with every cooling second of her own nakedness, yet she was loath to cover herself, to leave the intimacy of what had just happened behind—or, worse, pretend it had never happened... Just as Leo, perhaps, was pretending.

Or maybe he wasn't pretending. Maybe, for him, it had been just sex and she was the one, as always, who was constructing castles in the air—castles made of nothing, as insubstantial as smoke or mist, dissipating just as quickly.

He returned a few minutes later while she still lay there on the bed, naked and fighting against feeling exposed. She pushed her hair away from her eyes and struggled to a sitting position, still resisting the urge to cover herself. She'd promised herself—and, without his knowledge, Leo—

that she would be open to him tonight. That she wouldn't dissemble, guard or prevaricate. Not even now, when every instinct she possessed screamed for self-protection.

'Here.' His voice sounded alarmingly brusque as he pressed a bottle of water into her hands.

'Where—?'

'There's a mini-fridge in the dressing room.' The corner of his mouth quirked in what Alyse couldn't be sure was a smile. 'They put champagne in there as well, but I thought we'd had enough of that.'

'Ah. Yes.' *Because this wasn't a champagne-worthy moment?* She took a sip of the chilled water.

Leo drained half of his own before he lowered it from his lips, twisting the bottle around in his hands, his gaze averted from hers. Alyse just waited, sensing he intended to say something, but having no idea what it was.

Finally he lifted his gaze to meet hers, and even then she couldn't gauge his mood, couldn't fathom what he intended to say, or how he felt at all. He took a deep breath and let it out slowly. Alyse braced herself.

'I don't know,' he began haltingly, 'how much I have to give.'

Ayse just stared at him, his words slowly penetrating the dazed fog of her mind. *I don't know how much I have to give.* She felt a smile spread across her face—a ridiculously huge smile, considering what he'd said was a far, far cry from a declaration of love.

And yet it was something. It was a lot, for a man like Leo, because he was saying—at least, she hoped he was saying—that he still had *something* to give. And, more importantly, that he wanted to give it.

'That's okay,' she said softly and Leo glanced away.

'I'm sorry,' he said after a moment. 'For treating our marriage—our relationship—like an imposition.'

'That's what it was for you,' Alyse answered. She didn't add what everything inside her was hoping, singing: *until now.*

'I've never tried a real relationship before,' he continued, his gaze still averted. 'At least, not for a long while.'

'Neither have I.'

He glanced at her then, a slow smile curving his mouth. 'Then that makes two of us.'

She smiled back, her hopes soaring straight to the sky. 'I suppose it does.'

Neither of them spoke for a few moments and Alyse couldn't keep the lightness, the giddy relief, from swooping through her. She tried to tell herself that really this was very little, that she wasn't even sure what Leo was saying or offering. Yet still, the hope. The joy. She couldn't keep herself from feeling them, from wanting to feel them.

Eventually Leo took her half-empty water bottle as well as his own and put them away. Alyse slipped to the bathroom and returned to find him in bed, the firelight flickering over his bronzed body, his arms above his head. She hesitated on the threshold, still unsure how to act, and then Leo pulled aside the duvet and patted the bed.

'Come here,' he said softly and, smiling, she came.

She slid into the bed and felt her heart lurch with unexpected joy once again when he gently pulled her to him and cradled her body against his own, her head pillowed on his arm. She breathed in the scent of him, a woodsy after-shave and clean soap, and listened to the crackle of the logs in the fireplace and the steady beat of his heart against her cheek. She felt almost perfectly content.

Neither of them spoke, but the silence wasn't tense, strained or even awkward at all. It was a silence of new understanding. And, instead of pressing and longing for more, Alyse let this be enough. Lying in Leo's arms, it felt like everything.

CHAPTER TEN

WHEN SHE WOKE Leo was still stretched out beside her, a slight smile curving his mouth and softening his features. Alyse gazed at him unreservedly for a moment and then, feeling bold, brushed a kiss against that smiling mouth.

Leo's eyes fluttered open and his hands came up to her shoulders, holding her there against him.

'That's a rather nice way to wake up,' he said, and before she could respond he shifted her body so she was lying fully on top of him, the press of his arousal against her belly.

'I think you might have an even nicer way in mind,' she murmured as Leo slid his hand from her shoulder to her breast, his palm cupping its fullness.

'I certainly do,' he said, and neither of them spoke for a little while after that.

Later, when they'd showered and dressed and were eating breakfast in a private dining room,

Alyse asked him what his plans were for the day. Despite their morning love-making, in the bright light of day she felt some of her old uncertainties steal back. Perhaps Leo was content to enjoy their intimacy at night while still keeping himself apart during the day, consumed with work and royal duty.

Sitting across from him, sneaking glances at his stern profile, she was conscious of how little he'd said last night. *I don't know how much I have to give.* Really, in most relationships—if they even *had* a relationship—that would have been a warning, or at least a disclaimer. Not the promise she, in her naïvely and ridiculous hope, had believed it to be.

Leo considered her question. 'I have a meeting this morning with some Cabinet members about a new energy bill. But I'm free this afternoon. I thought—perhaps—I could give you a tour of the palace? You haven't actually seen much of it.'

Alyse felt a smile bloom across her face and some of those uncertainties scattered. Some, not all. Leo smiled back, a look of boyish uncertainty on his face.

'That sounds wonderful,' she said, and his smile widened, just as hers did.

They talked about other things then, a conversation that was wonderfully relaxed and yet also strangely new, exchanging views on films and books; relating anecdotes they'd never thought to share in the last six years. Simply getting to know one another.

After breakfast Leo excused himself to get ready for his meeting and Alyse went upstairs to unpack. She spent the morning in her room, catching up on correspondence and tidying her things before she went down to lunch.

Sophia had gone out for the day, thankfully, and Alessandro was otherwise occupied, so it was just her, Leo and Alexa at the lunch table.

'So how is married life, you two?' Alexa asked after the footman had served them all and retired. 'Bliss?'

Leo smiled faintly and shook his head. 'Don't be cynical, Lex.'

'*You're* telling *me* not to be cynical?'

'Wonders never cease,' Leo answered dryly, and Alexa raised her eyebrows.

'So marriage has changed you.'

Alyse held her breath as Leo took a sip of his water, his face thoughtful and yet also frustratingly blank. 'A bit,' he finally answered, not meeting anyone's gaze. Although she knew she shouldn't be, Alyse felt a rush of disappointment.

She took a steadying breath and focused on her own lunch. She knew she needed to be patient. Last night had changed things, but it was all still so new. She had to give it—*him, them*—time to strengthen and grow. Time for Leo truly to believe he *could* change.

Believe he could love.

After lunch Leo took her on a grand tour of the palace. They wandered through a dozen sun-dappled salons, empty and ornate, their footsteps echoing on the marble floors.

'This must have been great for hide and seek,' Alyse commented as they stood in one huge room decorated with portraits of his ancestors and huge pieces of gilt furniture. She tried to picture two dark-haired, solemn-eyed brothers playing in the room. Had Leo and his brother Alessandro been close? Had he missed him when he'd left? She had so many questions, but she knew Leo wasn't ready for her to ask them.

'I didn't really play in these rooms,' Leo answered, his hands shoved into his pockets, his gaze distant as he let it rove around the room. 'We were mostly confined to the nursery.'

'We?' Alyse prompted, and his expression didn't even flicker.

'The children. And of course, as I told you before, I went to boarding school when I was six.'

'That's rather young, isn't it? To go away.'

He shrugged. 'It was what my parents wanted.'

She thought of the remote King, the haughty Queen. Not the most loving of parents. 'Did you miss them?'

'No. You don't miss what you've never had.' She didn't think he was going to say anything more, but then he took a deep breath and continued, his gaze focused on the sunshine spilling through the window. 'If you've ever wondered how my parents got the idea of having us pretend to be in love, it's because that's all they've ever done. They were only interested in me or my— Or any of us when someone was watching.' His mouth twisted. 'A photo opportunity to show how much they loved us. As soon as it passed, they moved on.'

'But…' Alyse hesitated, mentally reviewing all the magazine inserts and commemorative books she'd seen about Maldinian's golden royal family: the posed portraits, the candid shots on the beach or while skiing. Everyone smiling, laughing.

Playing at happy families.

Was Leo really saying that his whole family life had been as much a masquerade as their engagement? She knew she shouldn't be surprised, yet she was. It was so unbearably soulless, so terribly cold.

No wonder Leo didn't believe in love.

Her heart ached for Leo as a boy, lonely and ignored. 'That sounds very lonely,' she said and he just shrugged.

'I'm not sure I know what loneliness is. It was simply what I was used to.' Yet she didn't believe that; she couldn't. What child didn't long for love and affection, cuddles and laughter? It was innate, impossible to ignore.

But not to suppress. Which was what it seemed Leo had done for his whole life, she thought sadly. Now her heart ached not just for Leo as a boy, but for the man he'd become, determined not to need anyone. Not to love anyone or want to be loved back—only to be let down.

'Anyway.' He turned from the window to face her, eyebrows raised. 'What about you? You're an only child. Did you ever want siblings?'

She recognised the attempt to steer the conversation away from himself and accepted it. He'd already revealed more than she'd ever anticipated or even hoped for. 'Yes, I did,' she admitted. 'But my parents made it clear there wouldn't be any more from a rather early age.'

'Why was that? Did they have trouble conceiving?'

'No. They just didn't want any more.' She saw the flicker of surprise cross his face and explained, 'They were happy with me—and mainly with each other. They were a real love match, you know. They may not be royalty, but they've still been featured in magazines. Their romance was a fairy tale.' Her voice came out a little flat, and Leo noticed.

'Your mother's some kind of American heiress, isn't she?'

'Her father owned a chain of successful hotels.

My uncle runs it now, but my mother was called the Brearley Heiress before she married.'

'And your father?'

'A French financier. They met at a ball in Paris—saw each other across a crowded room and that was it.' She gave him a rather crooked smile. 'You might not believe in love at first sight, but that's how it was for them.'

Leo didn't speak for a moment and when he finally did it was to ask, 'And growing up in the shadow of that…how was it for you?'

And with that telling question he'd gone right to the heart of the matter. 'Hard, sometimes,' Alyse confessed quietly. 'I love my parents, and I have no doubts whatsoever that they love me. But…it was always the two of them and the one of me, if that makes sense. They've always been wrapped up in each other, which is how it should be…'

She trailed off, realising belatedly how whingy she must sound, complaining about how much her parents loved each other. Leo had grown up in a household of bitterness and play-acting, and here she was saying her own home had had too much love? She felt ridiculous and ashamed.

'But it was lonely,' Leo finished softly. 'Or so I imagine, for a little girl on her own.'

'Sometimes,' she whispered. She felt a lump rise in her throat and swallowed hard. Leo reached for her hand, threading her fingers with his, and the simple contact touched her deep inside.

'Strange, how we grew up in two such different families and homes,' he murmured. 'Yet perhaps, in an odd way, our experience was just a little bit the same.'

'I can't complain, not really.'

'You weren't complaining. I asked a question and you answered it.' He drew her towards him, his one hand still linked with hers while the other tangled itself in her hair. 'But perhaps now we can put our families behind us. We'll start our own family, one day.' His smile was knowing and teasingly lascivious as he brushed her lips against his. 'Maybe today.'

'Maybe,' Alyse whispered shakily. They hadn't used birth control, hadn't even discussed it—and why should they? An heir was part of the package, part of her responsibility as Leo's bride and Maldinia's future queen.

Leo's baby.

She wanted it: him, the promise of a new family, a family created by love. Leo broke the kiss. *Patience.* This was still so new, still just a beginning.

But a wonderful one, and with a smile still on her lips she leaned forward and kissed him back.

Alyse gazed at her reflection in the mirror, smoothing the silver gown she was to wear for tonight's reception in one of London's most exclusive clubs. It had been four days since they'd returned from St Cristos, four wonderful days—and nights.

She still had to guard herself from leaping ahead, from longing for more than Leo was ready to offer. *I don't know how much I have to give.* And yet he *was* giving, and trying, and with every new conversation, every shared joke or smile, every utterly amazing night, she knew she was falling in love with him. Falling in love with the real him, the Leo she'd never even known.

She loved discovering that man, learning his habits, preferences and his funny little quirks, like the fact that he had to read the *entire* page of a newspaper, even the adverts, before turning to another; or that he liked chess but hated draughts.

And she loved learning the taut map of his body and hearing the shudder of pleasure that ripped through him when she kissed or touched him in certain places…

Just remembering made longing sweep through her body in a heated wave.

It hadn't all been perfect, of course. The strictures of palace life, of their royal appearances, had created moments of unspoken tension and Leo's inevitable emotional withdrawal. Just that morning they'd appeared in front of the palace to fly to London, and at the sight of the cheering crowds they'd both frozen before Alyse had started forward, smiling and waving.

'How is married life?' one young woman had asked her.

'More than I'd ever hoped for,' she'd answered.

The woman had beamed and Alyse had moved on, but she'd caught a glimpse of Leo out of the corner of her eye and uneasily noted his stony expression.

They didn't talk until they were in the royal jet, flying to London. Leo had snapped open his newspaper and, scanning the headlines, had re-marked, 'More than you'd ever hoped, eh?'

Alyse had blushed. 'Well...'

'Somehow I think you hope for a bit more,' he'd said softly, and her blush had intensified. She was trying so hard to be patient and accepting, but everything in her yearned for more. For love. Leo had glanced away. 'I don't know why,' he said, 'but the pretending feels harder now. More like a lie.'

Alyse understood what he meant. The de-ception cut deeper, now that there was actually something between them. Pretending you were in love when you felt nothing, as Leo had, was easier than when you felt just a little. She had a feeling their pretence was making Leo realise how little he still felt, and that wasn't a revela-tion she felt like discussing.

Sighing now, she turned away from the mir-ror. *Patience.*

A knock sounded on the door of her bedroom. Despite their honeymoon status, she and Leo had been given a royal suite with two bedrooms in the hotel where they were staying, and their luggage had been delivered to separate rooms. They'd dressed for the reception separately, Alyse with her small army of stylists hired by Queen Sophia and flown in from Paris.

'Are you ready?' Leo called from behind the door. 'The car is here.'

'Yes, I'm coming.' She opened the door, her breath catching at the sight of Leo at his most debonair and dignified in a white tie and tails. Then she saw the lines of tension bracketed from nose to mouth and fanning from his eyes. She couldn't ignore the stiltedness that had developed between them since they'd stepped back into the spotlight, and she didn't know how to overcome it. Everything between them felt too new and fragile to be tested like this.

Leo nodded in the direction of her fitted gown of silver satin; from a diamanté-encrusted halter-top it skimmed her breasts and hips and then flared out around her knees to fall in sparkly swirls to the floor. 'That's quite a gown. The stylists chose well.'

'I suppose they felt I needed to make a splash, since this is our first public appearance as husband and wife.'

'Yes, I have a feeling tonight will have us both

firmly in the spotlight.' Leo's mouth tightened and Alyse tried to smile.

'We did get a whole week away from it,' she said. 'And it's only one evening, after all.'

'One of many.' Leo slid his arm through hers. 'We should go. There are reporters outside.'

Once again flashbulbs went off in front of her as they stepped out of the hotel. Their car was waiting with several security guards to shepherd them from one door to another, but they paused on the threshold to smile and wave at the blurred faces in front of them. Leo's arm felt like a steel band under hers, his muscles corded with tension.

As they slid into the darkened sanctuary of the car, she felt him relax marginally, his breath coming out in a tiny sigh of relief.

'How have you stood it for so long?' she asked as she adjusted the folds of her dress around her. They were slippery to hold, and glittered even in the dim light of the car's interior.

'Stood what?'

'Being on display.'

He shrugged. 'It's all I've ever known.'

'But you don't like it.'

'I suppose I'm getting tired of it,' he allowed. 'It's been going on for a long time.'

'Since you were a child?'

'More or less.' He turned away from her then, so she could only see the shadowy profile of his cheek and jaw as he stared out of the window.

She couldn't imagine living like that for so long. The last six years had been challenging enough, with her intermittent public appearances, and she at least had had the escape of university and a relatively normal life. Leo never had, had never experienced anything really normal—or perhaps even real.

'We're here.'

The car had pulled up in front of one of London's exclusive clubs on Pall Mall, and another contingent of photographers and journalists waited by the doors.

They didn't pose for photographs or answer questions as the security hustled them from the car to the door, and then inside to the hushed foyer of the club. Yet even inside that hallowed place Alyse was conscious of a different kind of scrutiny: the hundred or so privileged guests who mingled in the club's ballroom were eyeing them with discreet but still noticeable curiosity. The Prince and his Cinderella bride; of course people were curious. Even alone in Durham she'd received those kinds of looks, had seen herself on the covers of magazines. She'd tried not to let it bother her, had made herself shrug it off and focus on the positives, on engaging with the public in as real a way as she could.

Yet she felt different now, and it wasn't because of the looks or the photos or the endless attention and publicity. It was because of Leo. She watched him out of the corner of her eye as he fetched them both champagne, talking and nodding with some important person, a stuffy-looking man with greying hair and a paunch. Alyse thought he looked vaguely familiar, but she didn't know his name.

And Leo… Leo looked remarkably at ease, the tension he'd shown earlier firmly masked and hidden away. He put his arm around her waist, and even as she thrilled to his touch, as always, Alyse felt a chill creep into her soul because how on earth could she actually tell when her husband was being real?

Perhaps the last week had been as much about

pretending as tonight. Perhaps Leo didn't even know *how* to be real.

'You need to smile,' Leo murmured, his own face set into easy, relaxed lines. 'You're looking tense.'

'Sorry.' Alyse tried to smile. This was so hard now, so much harder than it had ever been before. She was sick to death of pretending, sick of all this fear and uncertainty. Sick of wondering just what Leo felt for her, if anything.

'Now you look terrified,' Leo remarked in a low voice and she felt his arm tense around her waist. 'What's wrong? We've done this before.'

'It feels different now,' Alyse whispered. *She* felt different. But she had no idea if Leo did.

'It shouldn't,' he answered shortly, and steered her towards a crowd of speculative socialites. She forced herself to widen her wobbly smile, feeling more heartsick and uncertain than ever.

Leo fought the urge to tear off his white tie and stride from the club without a backward glance. Every second of this evening had been interminable, and the falseness of his and Alyse's behavior rubbed him horribly raw. He'd never minded before or, if he had, he'd shrugged it off. He'd had to. He'd *always* had to.

Yet now… Now the pretence irritated and even sickened him. The last week had been difficult at times, uncomfortable at others, but it had been real—or at least as real as he knew anything to be. The days and nights he'd spent with Alyse had fed something in him, a hunger he'd never known he had. He wanted more even as he doubted whether he should—or could.

He glanced again at Alyse, her eyes troubled even as she smiled at someone, and he desired nothing more in this moment than to take her in his arms and strip that shimmery gown from her body, let it slide into a silver puddle at her feet…

Her smile, he thought, looked decidedly wooden. Why was it so hard to pretend to be in love, when they'd been getting along better than ever? It should have been easier, but it wasn't. Friendship *had* complicated things, he thought darkly, just as he'd predicted. The parody of head-over-heels emotion they were enacting now only made their real relationship—whatever that was—seem paltry in comparison…and he had a feeling Alyse knew it.

I don't know how much I have to give. The words had come from him with sudden, startling honesty, because in that moment after they'd first made love he hadn't known what he was going to say, only that everything had changed.

But perhaps it hadn't changed. Perhaps even that had been nothing more than a mirage, a fantasy, just as tonight was. Everything in his life—every emotion, every caress, kiss or loving touch—had been faked. How on earth could he expect this to be real?

He didn't even know what real was.

Two hours later they were back in the car, speeding towards their hotel in Mayfair. All around them the lights of the city glittered under a midsummer drizzle, the pavement slick and gleaming with rain. Alyse hadn't spoken since they'd got into the car and Leo eyed her now, her face averted from him so he could only see the soft, sweet curve of her cheek, the surprising strength of her jaw. He longed to touch her.

He didn't.

This was their life now, he reminded himself. This pretending. No matter what might be developing between them, neither of them could escape the grim reality that every time they stepped outside of the palace they would be pretending to feel something else.

A simple, emotionless business arrangement would really be easier.

Yet, even as he told himself that, he couldn't keep from reaching for her as soon as they were back in their suite. She came willingly, her dress whispering against his legs, but he saw shadows in her eyes and her lip trembled before she bit it. He wanted to banish it all: the party, the pretence, the doubt and fear he felt in her now—and in himself. He wanted to make her smile, and the only way he knew of doing that was to kiss her, so he did.

Gently at first, but then he felt the softness of her mouth, the surrender of her sigh, and he drove his fingers into her hair, scattering all the diamond-tipped pins, as he pressed her against the wall of the foyer and devoured her with his kiss.

Alyse responded in kind and he felt a raw desperation in both of their need, a hunger to forget all the play-acting tonight and simply lose themselves in this—perhaps the only real thing they shared.

And lose himself he did, sliding his hands under the slippery satin of her gown, bunching it heedlessly about her hips as she wrapped her legs around his waist and he drove into her, lost himself inside her, his face buried in the warm curve of her neck as her body shook with pleasure.

They didn't speak afterwards and silently Leo led her from the foyer, leaving the hair pins and her shoes scattered on the floor. He peeled the dress from her body and shrugged off his own clothes before he drew her to the bed, wrapped his body around her and tried to shut out the world.

He woke several hours later, the room still swathed in darkness, and a glance at the clock told him it was an hour or so before dawn. He felt relentlessly awake and silently he slipped from Alyse's embrace, leaving her sleeping in his bed.

In the sitting room he powered up his laptop, determined to do a few hours' work before Alyse woke. They had engagements planned all day today, and they flew to Paris tonight for yet another reception, another full day tomorrow, yet another day of pretending. He pushed the thought away.

He would focus on work, the one thing that gave him satisfaction, a sense of purpose. He still needed to work on the wording of the bill for parliament regarding improvements to Maldinia's technological infrastructure, something his father had never remotely cared about.

He opened an Internet browser on his laptop to check his email and stopped dead when he saw that morning's news headline blaring across the screen:

Cinderella's Secret Lover Tells All.

Slowly he clicked on the article and scanned the first paragraph.

Prince Leo and his bride have always been the stuff of a fairy tale, and perhaps that's all it has been—for Matthew Cray, a student with the new princess at Durham University, has confessed to having a secret love affair with Alyse...

The game was up, Leo thought numbly. Everyone would know their relationship was fake, just as every relationship he'd ever had was fake. Sickened, he sat back in his chair. His mind spun with the implications of the article, the damage control that would need to be done—and quickly. But underneath the practicalities he felt something he hated to feel, didn't want to acknowledge now—the pain of hurt, the agonising ache of betrayal. He knew it wasn't fair; he'd forgiven Alyse, and it had been a long time ago anyway.

But seeing it all there on the page, knowing she'd convinced herself she loved him when she really hadn't...why should now be any different?

There's no such thing as love, he reminded himself brutally. *You've been playing at it this last week, but it's not real. It can't be.* And, swearing under his breath, he clicked on another glaring headline and began to read.

CHAPTER ELEVEN

'LEO?'

Alyse stood in the doorway of the bedroom, her gaze fastened on her husband and the stricken look on his face. He was staring blankly at the screen of his laptop, but as he heard her call his name he turned to her, his expression ironing out.

'What are you doing awake?'

'What are you?' She bit her lip. 'I woke up and wondered where you were.'

He gestured to his computer. 'Just getting a little work done. I couldn't sleep.'

Alyse took a step closer. Although Leo's face was implacable and bland now, she sensed the disquiet underneath. Something was wrong. 'What's happened?' she asked quietly.

'Nothing.'

'What were you looking at on the computer?'

'Just work—' He stopped, raking a hand through his hair. 'I suppose I'll have to tell you,' he said after a moment. 'We'll both have to deal with the damage control.'

Her stomach plunged icily. 'Damage control?'

Sighing, he clicked on the mouse and pointed to the screen. Alyse read the headline, everything in her freezing.

Cinderella's Secret Lover Tells All.

'Oh no,' she whispered. 'Oh no. How could he?'

'I imagine he was offered a great deal of money.'

'But it was years ago.' She stopped, swallowing hard, nausea rising in a roiling tide within her. She could just glimpse snatches of the awful article, phrases like 'drunken passion' and—heaven forbid—'marriage masquerade'.

She leaned forward, her eyes darting over the damning words.

According to Cray, Alyse and Prince Leonardo of Maldinia have simply been pretending to be in love to satisfy the public.

They knew. The whole world knew the truth about her and Leo. She stumbled back, one fist pressed to her lips, and Leo closed the laptop.

'I'm sorry,' she whispered and he shrugged.

'It was years ago. You have nothing to feel sorry for now.'

'But if I hadn't—'

'We'll deal with it,' he cut her off flatly. 'You should get dressed. I imagine we'll have to go back to Maldinia this morning to talk to the press office. We want a united front about how to handle this.'

He turned away and Alyse felt her insides twist with anxious misery. This was all her fault. And, while she accepted that Leo had forgiven her for her indiscretion from so many years ago, she feared their fragile relationship would not survive this ordeal.

With an icy pang of dread she remembered Queen Sophia's words: no use to Leo.

The worst had happened. She was a liability—to the monarchy and to Leo. And, if he didn't really feel anything for her, did he even want to stay married to her? What would be the point?

Miserably she went to shower and dress, her heart like lead inside her, weighing her down. The media frenzy would be excruciating, she knew. Who else would come forward to pick apart her university years? She might only have had that one lamentable experience, but she knew how the media worked, how people were tempted. Other stories would be made up; she could be depicted as a heartless, conniving slut.

And what about Leo? Her heart ached then not for herself, but for him. He'd have to deal with the shame and humiliation of being seen as the betrayed lover, the duped prince. She closed her eyes, forced the tears back. Recriminations would not serve either of them now.

Several grim-faced stylists were waiting when she emerged from the shower and they launched into a description of their strategy before she'd even taken the towel from her hair.

'You want to look muted and modest today, but not ashamed. Not like you have something to hide.'

'I don't have anything to hide,' Alyse answered before she could stop herself. 'Not any more.'

The stylists exchanged glances and ignored what she said. 'Subtle make-up, hair in a loose knot—earrings?'

'Pearl studs,' the other one answered firmly, and numbly Alyse let them go to work.

Forty-five minutes later she emerged into the sitting room where Leo was dressed in a charcoal-grey suit and talking on his mobile, his voice terse. Nervously Alyse fiddled with her earrings, her heart seeming to continually lurch up into her throat. She'd always managed to handle the press before, but then they'd always been on her side. How hard was it, really, to smile and wave for people who seemed to adore you?

Today would be different. She'd turned on the television while the stylists were organising her outfit and had seen that Matt's interview was breaking news even on the major networks. Ridiculous, perhaps, but still true. They'd managed to dig up a photo of her walking to lectures with him and, innocent as it had been then, it looked damning. She had her hand on his arm and her head was tilted back as she laughed. She didn't even remember the moment; she'd only walked with him a couple of times. They hadn't even been that good friends, she thought miserably, but who would believe that now? The media was implying she'd indulged in a long, sordid affair.

'No need for that,' one stylist, Aimee, had said

crisply, and turned off the TV. 'Let's get you dressed.'

Now as she waited for Leo to finish his call—he was speaking in rapid Italian too fast for her to understand—Alyse smoothed the muted blue silk of her modest, high-collared dress, a satin band of deeper blue nipping in her waist. 'Virgin blue', the colour was apparently called. How unfitting.

Finally Leo disconnected the call and turned to her, his brows snapping together. 'A good choice,' he said, nodding towards her dress. 'The jet is waiting.'

'The jet? Where are we going? What's—what's going to happen?'

'We're heading back to Maldinia. I considered keeping our heads high and honouring the rest of our engagements in Paris and Rome, but I don't think that's the best course of action now.'

'You don't?'

Leo shook his head, the movement brisk and decisive. 'No. I think the best thing is to come clean. Admit what happened and that I've forgiven you. Keep it firmly in the past.'

'And how...?'

'I've arranged for us to do a television interview.'

'A television interview?' Alyse repeated sickly. She might have been on the cover of dozens of magazines, but she'd never actually been on TV. The thought of being on it now, a public confessional, made her head spin and her nerves strain to breaking. 'But—'

'I'll explain it all on the plane,' Leo said. 'We need to get going.'

The outside of the hotel was mobbed with paparazzi and the security guards had to fight their way through to get to them as they waited at the door.

Alyse ducked her head as she came out, Leo's arm around her, flashbulbs exploding in her face, questions hammering her heart.

'Did you ever love Leo, Alyse?'

'How long were you seeing Matthew Cray?'

'Have there been others?'

'Was it for money or fame, this marriage masquerade?'

'Do you have any conscience at all?'

She closed her eyes, her heart like a stone inside her as Leo and the security guard guided her into the waiting limo. As soon as the doors had closed she let out a shaky sigh of relief, halfway to a sob.

'That was awful.'

Leo turned away from the window, his face expressionless. 'It will get worse.'

'I know.' She took a deep breath, let it fill her lungs before releasing it slowly. She still felt shaky from her first encounter with a malevolent press—one of many, she had no doubt. 'Leo, I'm so sorry this has happened. I know it's my fault.'

'As far as I can tell, it's Matthew Cray's fault.'

'But if I hadn't—'

'Alyse, you can beat yourself up all you like about what happened years ago, but it doesn't change things now, so really there's no point.' His expression didn't soften as he added, 'And I don't want you to. I know you're sorry. I understand you regret it.'

'But—but do you forgive me?'

'There's nothing to forgive.'

She should have been comforted by his words, but she wasn't. He spoke them so emotionlessly, his face so terribly bland; any intimacy they'd once shared seemed utterly lost in that moment.

Cold, stern, unyielding Leo was back, and she had no idea how to find the man she'd begun to fall in love with. Perhaps he didn't exist any more; perhaps he'd never existed.

Weary and heartsick, Alyse leaned her head back against the seat and closed her eyes.

Leo gazed at Alyse, her face pale, her eyes closed, and felt a needling of guilt mixed with an unexpected pang of sympathy. After being adored by the press for six years, it had to be hard to be cast as the villain.

Not that *he'd* ever cared what the media thought of him one way or the other. Perhaps Alyse didn't care either. Perhaps it was simply guilt that made her look so tired and wretched.

Leo knew he should have tried harder to comfort her. He probably should have held her and told her not to worry, that they'd get through this together. That none of it mattered. He hadn't done any of that; he hadn't thought of doing it until now, when it felt too late. He simply didn't have it in him.

I don't know how much I have to give. No, he sure as hell didn't. Ever since the news of Alyse's indiscretion had broken he'd felt his fragile emotions shutting down, the familiar retreat into cold silence. It was safer, easier, and it was what he knew. And he also knew it was hurting Alyse. He supposed that was a step in the right direction; at least he was aware he was hurting her.

But he still didn't have the ability, or perhaps just the strength, to stop it.

Alyse opened her eyes, her gaze arrowing in on him. 'Tell me about this television interview,' she said and Leo nodded, glad to escape his thoughts.

'It's with Larissa Pozzi,' he said and Alyse blanched.

'But she's—'

'Broadcast on all the major networks. We need the publicity.' Alyse just shook her head, and Leo knew what she wasn't saying. Larissa relished scandal and melodrama, was always handing her guests tissues with her overly made-up face in a moue of false sympathy. Being interviewed by her was a necessary evil; he had chosen it because it would get their message across to the most people most quickly.

'And what are we meant to say?' Alyse asked.

'That we'd had a fight and you were foolish.

You've regretted it deeply ever since and I've known all along and forgave you ages ago.' He spoke tonelessly, hating every lie that he'd come up with with the approval of the royal press office. Hating that, even in telling a bit of the truth, they were still perpetuating a lie. And he was sick to the death of pretending. Of lies.

He could not imagine saying them on live television. Every word would stick in his throat like a jagged glass shard. He wanted to be done with deception, with pretence, for ever, even as he recognised how impossible it was.

Alyse's face had gone chalk-white and she glanced away. 'I see,' she murmured, and he knew she did: more lies. More pretending. They would never be done with them, never have the opportunity to be real.

So how on earth could they have any kind of real relationship in that toxic environment, never mind love?

Not that he loved her. He didn't even know what love was.

Did he?

The question reverberated through him. The last week had been one of the sweetest of his life, he had to admit. The memory of Alyse's smile, the sweet slide of her lips against his, how he'd felt when he'd been buried inside her…

If that wasn't love, it was something he'd never experienced before. It was intense and over-whelming, addictive and, hell, frightening.

But was it love?

Did it even matter?

'Why don't you get some rest?' Leo said brusquely. 'You look completely washed out, and we'll be there in another hour.'

And, putting those troubling questions firmly to the back of his mind, he reached for his attaché and some paperwork that needed his attention.

Alyse's stomach clenched as they stepped off the royal jet and were ushered quickly into the wait-ing limo with its accompanying motorcade of security. They were to go directly to the palace for a press briefing, and then the television inter-view that would take place in one of the palace's private apartments. Alyse dreaded both events. She dreaded the condemnation she'd see on ev-eryone's faces, from King Alessandro to Queen Sophia to the cloying Larissa Pozzi…to Leo.

He'd said there was nothing to forgive, but his stony face told otherwise. She had no idea what he was really thinking or feeling, and she was desperately afraid to ask. That was how fragile and untried their feelings for each other were, she acknowledged with a wry despair. It couldn't face up to a moment's honesty, never mind any hardship or scrutiny.

The press secretary, along with the Queen, were waiting for them as soon as they stepped into the palace. Alyse's stomach plunged straight to her toes as they entered one of the smaller receiving rooms. Queen Sophia stood at one end in all of her icy, regal splendour.

'Mother.' Leo's voice was toneless as he went forward to kiss his mother's cheek. She didn't offer any affection back or even move, and despite the nerves jangling inside her Alyse felt a kind of sorrowful curiosity at the dynamic between mother and son.

Queen Sophia swung her cold blue gaze to Alyse. 'This is a disaster,' she said, 'as I'm sure you're aware. A complete disaster.'

'It's under control—' Leo began tightly, but his mother cut across him.

'Do you really think so, Leo?' Her voice rang out scornfully but Leo didn't react. 'People will believe what they want to believe.'

'They've always wanted to believe in Alyse,' he answered quietly. 'They've always loved her.'

'And they'll be just as quick to hate her,' Sophia snapped. 'That's the nature of it, of publicity.'

'Then I have to wonder why we've always been so quick to court it,' Leo responded coolly. 'Oh, I remember now—because you needed the positive press. You've needed Alyse, to make up for all the selfish choices you and Father have made over the years.'

'How dare you?' Sophia breathed.

'I dare,' Leo answered, 'because you've been using me and then Alyse—using everyone you can—to make up for your own deficiencies. I won't have you blaming us for them now. We'll handle this, Mother, and you need not concern yourself at all.'

Sophia's eyes glinted malice. 'And what happens when they hate her, Leo? What happens when it all falls apart?'

Ice slid down Alyse's spine. *When they had no use for her.*

'We'll deal with that possibility when and if it happens,' Leo answered, and turned away.

Sophia whirled away from them both. 'I'll send Paula in,' she said tightly, and with a slam of the doors she was gone.

'Thank you,' Alyse said quietly, 'for defending me. Even if I don't deserve it.'

'You do deserve it. Enough with the *mea culpa* bit, Alyse.'

'I'm sorry.'

'You're still doing it.'

She smiled wanly. 'Habit, I guess.'

'I'm not angry,' Leo said after a moment. 'At least, not at you. I might be harbouring a little rage for the paparazzi, but I can't really blame them either. They're just doing their job and we've been feeding their frenzy for years now.'

'And you're sick of it.'

'Yes.' He lapsed into silence, his forehead furrowed into a frown as he gazed out of the palace windows at acres of manicured lawn. Alyse watched him warily, for she sensed some conflict in him, something he wanted to say—but did she want to hear it?

'Alyse…' he began, but before he could say any

more Paula bustled in with a sheaf of papers in one manicured hand.

'Now, we need to go over just what you'll say.'

'It's under control,' Leo said shortly. 'I know what I'm going to say.'

Paula looked surprised, a little insulted. 'But I'm meant to brief—'

'Consider us briefed,' Leo answered. 'We're ready.'

Alyse fought down nausea. She didn't feel remotely ready, and frankly she could use a little help from Paula. 'What are we going to say?' she whispered as they headed towards the suite where the interview would take place. 'I could use—'

'Leave it to me.'

'But—'

'Let's go in,' he said, and ushered her into the reception room with its cameras and lights already set up. 'They're waiting.'

The interview, at least at first, was a blur to Alyse. She shook Larissa Pozzi's hand and the woman, all glossy nails and too-white teeth, gushed over the two of them.

'Really, we're doing this for you,' she said, laying a hand on Alyse's arm, her long, curved nails digging into her skin. 'The world wants to hear your side of the story.'

'My side,' Alyse repeated numbly. It didn't sound good—that there were already sides, battle lines clearly drawn.

Assistants prepped them both for make-up and hair as they sat on a sofa facing Larissa and the cameras. Alyse could feel the tension coming off Leo in waves and, though he managed to convey an air of relaxation, chatting easily with Larissa, she knew he was beyond tense.

She *knew* him. She knew him now more than ever before, and that was both comforting and thrilling—that this man was no longer a stranger but someone she knew and—*loved*?

Did she love him? Had she fallen in love that quickly, that easily? And yet nothing about the last week or so had been easy. It had been wonderful, yes, but also painful, emotional, tense and fraught. And still the best time of her life.

She just prayed it wasn't over, that this wasn't the beginning of the end. Glancing at Leo's profile, his jaw taut even as he smiled, she had no idea if that was the case.

'We're just about ready,' Larissa told them both as she positioned herself in her chair, and if anything Alyse felt Leo become even tenser, although his position didn't change.

Three, two, one...

'So, Prince Leo, we're so thrilled to have you on the show,' Larissa began in her gushing voice. Alyse felt her smile already become a rictus, her hands clenched tightly together in her lap and a bead of sweat formed at her hairline under the glare of the lights and cameras. 'And of course everyone is dying to hear your side of the story... as well as your bride's.' The talk show hostess's gaze moved speculatively to Alyse, and she didn't think she was imagining the glint of malice in those over-wide eyes. No matter how Larissa gushed to Leo, Alyse knew she'd still be cast as the scarlet woman. It made for a juicy story.

'Well, it's really rather simple, Larissa,' Leo began in a calm, even voice. He had one arm stretched along the back of the sofa, his fingers grazing Alyse's shoulder. 'When that photograph was taken all those years ago—and you know the photo I mean, of course.'

'Of *course.*'

'Alyse and I barely knew each other. We'd only just met that very evening, actually.'

'But you looked so in love,' Larissa said, eyes widening even more. She glanced rather accusingly at Alyse, who only just managed to keep her smile in place. Nothing about that photo, she thought, had been deliberately faked. It was, perhaps, the one honest moment the press had actually captured between her and Leo.

Leo lifted a shoulder in a 'what can I say?' shrug and Larissa let out a breathy sigh. 'But it was love at first sight, Prince Leo, wasn't it? You haven't actually been faking your engagement all these years, as people are so cruelly suggesting?'

Smiling, he held up one hand, his wedding ring glinting on his finger. 'Does that look fake to you?'

'But your *feelings*...'

'Alyse's and my marriage was always one of convenience,' Leo said and Alyse stiffened in shock. She had a feeling this would not have been part of Paula's brief.

Larissa drew back in exaggerated shock. 'Convenience? No! Not the prince and his Cinderella bride?'

Leo just smiled and shrugged. 'Royal marriages often are.'

'But you've been portrayed as being so in love, an inspiration to couples—as well as singles—everywhere.'

'And we are in love,' Leo replied steadily. 'Now.' A moment of silence spun out as Larissa stared at him; Alyse stared at him. *What was he saying?*

'It took a long time for those feelings to come, especially on my part,' he continued in that same steady voice. 'But they have come, and that's really the important thing, don't you think? Not what happened—or didn't happen—before.' He let this sink in for a moment before continuing. 'The main thing—the beautiful thing—is that I love Alyse now. I've fallen in love with my wife.'

And then he turned to her, while Alyse tried not to gape like a fish, and gave her a smile that felt both private and tender, and was being broadcast to a billion people around the world.

A smile that was surely a lie...wasn't it? Wasn't he just pretending, as always?

'Alyse, you look surprised,' Larissa said and,

blinking, Alyse tried to focus on the talk-show hostess rather than her husband.

'Not surprised so much as thrilled,' she managed, barely aware of what she was saying. 'And so happy. I admit, it's been a rocky road to get to where we are. Leo and I have always been committed to marriage, but love isn't something you can force.'

Larissa pursed her lips. 'Let's talk about Matthew Cray.'

'Let's not,' Leo interjected swiftly. 'Whatever happened was a single moment many years ago, and not worth our time or discussion. As I've said before, what matters is now—and our future.' Again he smiled at Alyse, but this time she looked into his eyes. They looked dark and hard and her heart quailed within her. He didn't look like a man in love. She could feel the tension thrumming through him and her insides roiled. He was faking; of course he was. This was just another part of the pretence, and she was a fool for thinking otherwise even for a second.

She didn't remember the rest of the interview; her mind was spinning too much and Leo did most of the talking.

After an interminable half-hour they were done and Larissa and her crew were packing up. Leo ushered her from the filming area, one hand firmly on her elbow.

'Hopefully that did the trick,' he said, and that last frail hope died.

'A very clever way to spin it,' she managed and Leo gave her a sudden, penetrating look.

'Is that how you saw it?'

She stared at him, longing to ask him what he meant, but so afraid to. Afraid to trust his feelings, or even hers. *What was real?* 'I…I don't know.'

'Prince Leo… Your Highness.' Leo turned and Alyse saw one of his father's aides hurrying towards him.

'Yes?'

'Your father requests your presence in his private study immediately.'

Leo frowned. 'Is something wrong?'

The aide looked uncomfortable as he answered, 'Prince Alessandro has arrived at the palace.'

Leo went completely still, his face draining of colour, and Alyse felt shock blaze through him. Prince Alessandro…Leo's brother. He'd returned.

Leo swallowed and then his expression ironed out. 'I'm coming,' he said shortly, and walked away from Alyse.

CHAPTER TWELVE

SANDRO WAS HERE. Leo blinked, still finding it hard to believe his brother was here, just a room away. He'd come home. After fifteen years away—a decade and a half of complete silence—he'd returned, the prodigal son. Leo could not untangle the knot of emotions that had lodged inside him, rose in his throat. Fear, anger, confusion, disbelief…and, yes, love and joy.

Too much.

He was tired of feeling so damn much. After years of schooling himself not to feel anything, not to care or want or allow himself to be hurt, it was all coming out—just like it had during that interview.

I've fallen in love with my wife.

What on earth had made him say such a thing? Made him confess it—if it were even true? The words had spilled out of him, needing to be said, burning within him. Now he fought against such an admission, attempting, quite desperately, to claw back some self-protection. Some armour.

And now Sandro.

'Leo...' Alyse hurried after him. 'Why is Sandro here?'

He turned to stare at her. 'You know about Sandro?'

'Your mother told me a few days ago.'

He shook his head, unable to untangle his emotions enough to know how he felt about Alyse knowing and not saying a word. This was intimacy? Honesty?

'Let's not talk about this here,' he said. 'My father is expecting me.' She followed him to his father's study but he barred her at the door. 'This meeting is private, Alyse. I'll talk to you after.' He knew he sounded cold and remote, but he couldn't help it. That was who he was. Everything else had been an aberration. A mistake.

A mistake he would miss.

'I'll see you later.'

She bit her lip, her eyes wide with fear and uncertainty, but then she slowly nodded. 'Okay,' she whispered, and slowly walked down the hall.

Leo knocked once and then opened the door to

his father's most sacred room, his private study, and stared directly into the face of his older brother.

Alessandro. Sandro. The only person he'd ever felt was a true friend, who understood him, accepted him. Loved him. He looked the same, and yet of course so much older. His unruly dark hair had a few silver threads, the strands catching the light and matching the grey glint of his eyes. He was taller and leaner than Leo, possessing a sinewy, charismatic grace, just as he had at twenty-one when Leo had last seen him.

Don't go, Sandro. Don't leave me alone. Please.

He'd begged and Sandro had gone.

'Leo.' Sandro nodded once, his expression veiled, and Leo nodded back. Quite the emotional reunion, then.

'I've summoned Alessandro back to Maldinia,' King Alessandro said with the air of someone who trusted his innate authority.

'So I see.' Leo cleared his throat. 'It's been a long time, Sandro.'

'Fifteen years,' his brother agreed. His silver gaze swept over him, telling him nothing. 'You look well.'

'As do you.' And then they lapsed into silence, these brothers who had once, despite the
six years' difference in their ages, been nearly
inseparable—compatriots as children, banding
together as they had determinedly tried to ignore
their parents' vicious fights and sudden, insen-
sible moments of staged affection.

Later they'd gone to the same boys' boarding
school and Sandro had become Leo's champion,
his hero, a sixth former to his first year, cricket
star and straight-A pupil. Yet always with the
time, patience and affection for his quieter, shyer
younger brother. Until he'd decided to leave all
of it—and him—behind.

Childish memories, Leo told himself now. In-
fantile thoughts. Whatever hero worship he'd had
for his brother, he'd long since lost it. He didn't
care any more, hadn't for years. The damnable
lump in his throat was simply annoying.

'Alessandro has agreed to return to his rightful place,' his father said and Leo's gaze swung
slowly to the King.

'His rightful place,' he repeated. 'You mean…?'

'When I am gone, he will be King.'

Leo didn't react. He made sure not to. He kept

completely still, not even blinking, even as inside he felt as if he'd staggered back from a near-fatal blow. In one swoop his father had taken his inheritance, his *reason*, away from him. For fifteen years he'd worked hard to prove he was worthy, that he would be a good king. He'd sacrificed desire for duty, had shaped his life to become the next monarch of Maldinia.

And just like that, on his father's whim, he wouldn't be. He turned to Sandro, saw his brother's lips twist in a grimace of a smile.

'So you're off the hook, Leo.'

'Indeed.' Of course his brother would see it that way. His brother had never wanted to be king, had walked away from it all, hating both the artifice and the pretension of royal life. He'd forged his own path in California; had started a highly successful IT firm, or so Leo's Internet searches had told him. And now he was leaving that all behind to return, to take Leo's place?

And leave Leo with…nothing?

Not even a wife. There was, he realised hollowly, no reason at all for him and Alyse to be married. To stay married. A week or so of fragile feeling surely didn't justify a life sentence. She would want to be free and so would he.

He *did*. He would.

He turned back to his father, unable to miss the cold glitter of triumph in the King's eyes. 'So how did this come to pass?' he asked in as neutral a tone as he could manage.

'I've always wanted Alessandro to be King,' his father answered shortly. 'It is his birthright, his destiny. You've known that.'

Of course he had, just as he'd known he was a poor second choice. He'd simply thought he'd proved himself enough in the last fifteen years to make up for the deficiency of being born second.

'And after this latest debacle...' King Alessandro continued, his lips twisting in contempt. 'All the work we've done has been destroyed in one careless moment, Leo.' *The work* we've *done?* Leo wanted to answer. *To shout.*

His father had done nothing, *nothing* to restore the damn monarchy. He'd let his son—his second son—do all the work, shoulder all the responsibility. He said nothing. He knew there was no point.

The King drew himself up. 'Bringing Alessandro back will restore the monarchy and its reputation, its place at the head of society. New blood, Leo, fresh air. And we can forget about what happened with you and Alyse.'

Forget them both, tidy them away just as his father had done with Alessandro all those years ago. Move onto the next chapter in this damnable book.

But he didn't want to move on. He wouldn't have his life—his love—treated as no more than an unfortunate mistake. He didn't care so much about being king, Leo realised with shock, as being Alyse's husband. *I've fallen in love with my wife.* And it didn't matter any more.

Alyse didn't love him, not really. She might have convinced herself once, and she'd probably do so again, but it wasn't real. It wouldn't last, just as nothing had been real or lasting in his life.

Why should he trust this? Her? Or even himself, his own feelings that might vanish tomorrow?

'The matter is finished,' King Alessandro stated. 'Alessandro has accepted his birthright. He will return to live in Maldinia and take up his royal duties.'

Without waiting for a reply, the King left the

room, left the two brothers alone as a silence stretched on between them.

'He's still the same,' Sandro said after a moment, his voice flat and almost uninterested. 'Nothing's really changed.'

Everything's changed. Everything has just changed for me. Leo swallowed the words, the anger. He didn't want to feel it; there was no point. He wouldn't be king; he had no wife. 'I suppose,' he said.

'I'll need you, if you're willing,' Sandro said. 'You can pick whatever post you want. Cabinet minister?' He smiled, and for the first time Leo saw warmth in his brother's face, lighting his eyes. 'I've missed you, Leo.'

Not enough to visit, or even write. But then, he hadn't either. First he'd been forbidden, and then later he'd told himself he didn't care.

Now grief for all he'd lost rushed through him and he turned his face away, afraid Sandro would see all he felt in his eyes. 'Welcome back, Sandro,' he said when he trusted himself to speak and then he left the room.

Alyse paced the sitting room of the apartment they'd been given in one wing of the palace, her hands clenched, her stomach clenched, every-thing inside her taut with nerves. Her worries and uncertainties about the TV interview, and what Leo had said, had been replaced with the fear of what Sandro's return would mean for Leo—and her.

For she'd had a terrible certainty, as she'd watched Leo head for his father's study like a man on his way to the gallows, that everything had changed.

The door opened and she whirled around.

'Leo.'

His mouth twisted in what Alyse suspected was meant to be a smile but didn't remotely come close. 'It seems,' he said, striding towards the window, 'that we're both off the hook.'

'Off the *hook*? What do you mean? What's hap-pened, Leo? Why has Sandro come back?'

'My father summoned him.'

Alyse stared at him, saw the terrible coldness, almost indifference, on his face. 'Why did he leave in the first place?'

Leo shrugged and turned away. 'He hated royal life. Hated the way we always pretended and hated the burden of becoming king. He went to university, and when he received his diploma he decided to trade it all in for a life of freedom in the States.'

There was something that Leo wasn't saying, Alyse knew. Many things. He spoke tonelessly, but she felt his bitterness, his rage and even his hurt. She took a step closer to him. 'And why were you never in touch?'

'My parents forbade it. You don't walk away from royalty, especially not when you've been groomed to be king for your entire life.'

Shock blazed coldly through her as she realised what he was saying. 'So when he walked away, you were the heir.'

'Were,' Leo repeated. 'Yes.'

His voice was toneless, yet to Alyse he still sounded so bleak. She knew this man, knew when he was angry or happy or hurt. And right now she wanted to help him...if only she knew how. 'Leo, talk to me. Turn around and look at me, please. What's happened? Why are you so...?'

'I'm not anything,' he answered, and he turned around to look at her, his face as blank as his voice. 'I told you, Alyse, we're both off the hook.'

'I don't understand why you're saying that. What it means.'

'I'm off the hook for becoming king,' Leo explained slowly, as if she were a dim-witted child. 'And you're off the hook for being married to me.'

As if her wits were truly affected, it took her a few seconds to realise what he meant. 'What does your brother have to do with our marriage?' she whispered.

'Everything and nothing. Admittedly, I doubt he even knew I was married, but since he's accepted his birthright once more I'm no longer heir to the throne. Our marriage was a royal alliance, admittedly a forced one due to all the media attention. But there are no more reasons, Alyse.' He spread his hands wide, eyebrows raised in expectation. 'The media has sussed us out, and I'm not even going to be king in the first place. So it doesn't matter what either of us do.'

'And just what is it,' Alyse asked, her voice shaking, 'that you *want* to do?'

He lowered his brows, his expression flattening out. 'I see no reason for either of us to stay in a sham of a marriage.'

A sham of a marriage. She thought of what he'd said on air, how it had filled her for a few moments with a wary hope. A hope she hadn't quite been able to let go of, even now. *I've fallen in love with my wife.* Obviously he'd been spinning more lies to Larissa Pozzi, just as everything had been lies, perhaps even this last week or so.

'So you're suggesting a divorce,' she said flatly and for a moment Leo didn't respond.

'It seems sensible,' he finally said and a sudden, choking rage filled her, made her unable to speak.

'You bastard,' she finally managed, her voice thick with tears. 'Have you meant *anything* you've ever said? Do you even know how to be real or honest or *anything*?'

'Probably not.'

Alyse pressed her fists to her eyes and drew a shuddering breath. Now was not the time for tears. She'd have plenty of time, endless amounts, later to weep, to mourn. 'Leo.' She dropped her hands and forced herself to meet his cold, blank gaze. 'What about these last few weeks? What about how things changed between us, about how you said—'

'How I didn't know how much I had to give?' he filled in, a mocking edge to his voice. 'Well, now I do, and it turns out it's not all that much.'

'Why are you doing this?' she whispered. 'When just last night—'

'That was last night.' He swung around sharply, his hands jammed in his pockets as he stared out the window once more.

'And the fact that you won't be king changes your feelings towards me?' Alyse asked helplessly. 'I don't understand how that happens—'

'It was a *week*, Alyse. Ten days at most.' His voice echoed through the room with the sharp report of a rifle as he turned back to face her. 'A single bloody week. And yes, there were very nice parts, and the intensity made both of us think it could turn into more, which is understandable. We were looking at a marriage, after all, and trying to find a way to make it work.'

'We're still looking at a marriage—'

'No,' he answered flatly, 'we're not.'

It was like hammering on an iron door, she thought hopelessly, battering her fists and her heart against a stone wall. There was simply no way inside him, no way to understand what was going on behind that cold mask.

'Don't do this, Leo,' she whispered, her voice breaking. 'Please.' He gave no answer, not even a flicker of emotion in his eyes or a grimacing twist of his mouth. 'So what is meant to happen now?' she asked, her voice turning to raw demand. 'Am I just meant to…leave? Are you kicking me out?'

'Of course not. You may stay in the palace as long as you like. I'll leave.'

'Where will you—'

'It hardly signifies. I'll send you the paperwork.'

Alyse stared at him, those stern, hard features she'd come to know so well. Those mobile lips she'd kissed, the body she'd touched…*the heart she loved*.

She loved him, she knew that now, felt it inside her like a shining gold light, and Leo was doing his damnedest to extinguish it. They'd been married for ten days.

'Please,' she said one last time, and he didn't reply. Didn't move, didn't even blink. Taking a deep, shuddering breath, Alyse slowly turned and walked out of the room.

She walked down the corridor with its crystal chandeliers and sumptuous carpet, barely aware of her surroundings, or the liveried footmen standing to attention as she came to the top of the double staircase that led down into the palace's entrance hall. Her mind was spinning and she tasted acid in her mouth. Swallowing hard, she sank onto a spindly little gilt bench, her head in her hands.

'Your Highness—' One of the footmen started forward in concern.

'Just leave me,' she whispered, her head still in her hands. 'Please.' The footman stepped back. Alyse tried to marshal her thoughts. What would she do now? Where would she go? Her entire life, since she was eighteen years old and little more than a naïve child, had been oriented towards being Leo's wife, Maldinia's queen, and now that was taken away from her she was left spinning in a void of uncertainty.

Why was he doing this? Why didn't he believe their marriage was worth saving, that she loved him?

Just like you loved him when you were eigh-teen? When you told him you loved him, and then took it back? And haven't told him since, haven't trusted that any of this is real?

Could she really blame Leo for doubting not just his feelings, but her own? *She'd* doubted them. She'd insisted she was in love with him once, only for him to prove her disastrously wrong. Was it any wonder he doubted? His whole life people had been telling him they loved him—his parents, his brother, and they'd all, in their own way, been liars.

Why should he think she was any different?

She straightened, her gaze unseeing as thoughts tumbled through her mind. Did she love him now, a real, strong love, not the girlish fancy of be-fore? She felt the answer in her heart, beating with strong, sure certainty.

Yes.

And she'd never told him. She'd begged him to change his mind, had acted as if it was all up to him, when she was the one who needed to take control. Who could be strong.

Her legs felt shaky as she stood up and walked

slowly back to the apartment where she knew Leo waited. Where her heart, her whole life, waited.

Taking a deep breath, letting the air buoy her lungs, she opened the door and stepped into the room.

Leo sat on the bed, his elbows braced on his knees, his head lowered. Alyse's heart ached at the sight of his wretchedness even as new hope flickered to life within her heart. This wasn't a man unaffected by what just happened, the man who had coldly stared her down and almost—almost—won.

'Leo.'

He looked up, blinking as if she were an apparition. Alyse saw grief etched in the lines of his face before he deliberately blanked his expression. She knew how he did that now. She was starting to understand why. 'What are you doing here?'

'I want to finish our conversation.'

'I think our conversation is quite finished, Alyse. There's nothing more to say.'

'I have something more to say.'

'Oh?' He arched one eyebrow, coldly skeptical, but Alyse knew it was only a mask. At least, she hoped it was only a mask, that underneath the stern coldness beat the heart of the warm, generous man she'd come to know—and love. Yet even now fear and doubt skittered along her spine, crept into her mind. She forced them back.

'You told me once you wanted there to be no lies or pretence between us.' He jerked his head in a tiny nod, and Alyse made herself continue despite the fear coursing through her veins. 'And I don't want there to be either. So if you're going to dissolve our marriage, ask for a divorce, then you need to give me the real reason.'

'I did give you the real reason.'

'I don't think you did.'

His mouth tightened. 'That's not my problem, Alyse.'

'No, it's mine. Because I haven't been honest either. I've been so afraid—afraid of losing you by pushing too hard or asking for too much. And afraid of my own feelings, if I could trust them.' He didn't respond, but she saw a wary alertness in his eyes and knew he was listening. Emboldened, she took a step forward. 'I really did believe I loved you all those years ago, you know,' she said softly. 'And then when I started to get to know you properly, I began to doubt the feelings I'd had…just as you doubted them.' She hesitated, wanting to be honest yet needing to search for the words. 'It was a terrible feeling, to realise I'd fooled myself for so long. It made me wonder if I could ever trust my feelings—my own heart—again. Or if anyone else could. Like you.'

Still nothing from him, but Alyse kept on. She sat next to him on the bed, her thigh nudging his, needing his touch, his warmth. 'I've come to understand just a little how you must have endured the same thing. Your parents telling you they love you, but only for the cameras. Not really meaning it.' She waited, but he didn't answer. 'And your brother too—leaving you like that. You were close, weren't you?'

His throat worked and he glanced away. 'Yes,' he said, and his voice choked.

She laid a hand on his arm. 'For your whole life people have been letting you down, Leo, pretending they love you and then doing something else. Is it any wonder you're afraid of relationships, of love, now? I'm afraid and I didn't have that experience.'

'I'm not afraid—'

'Don't lie to me. Love is scary, even when you don't have the kind of emotional baggage you do. Or I do, for that matter. Pretending we're in love for six years didn't do either of us any favours.'

'That's why I want this marriage to end. No more pretending. No more lies.'

Alyse drew a deep breath. 'So you'd be telling the truth if you said you didn't feel anything for me?' No answer, but at least a vigorous *yes* hadn't sprung to his lips. 'Because I wouldn't. I do feel something for you, Leo. Something I didn't trust at first because of everything that had gone before. And maybe I'm still not exactly sure what love is, what it feels like, but with every moment I'm with you I believe I feel it for you.' She took another breath and let it out slowly. 'I love you, Leo.'

He let out a short, hard laugh. 'I've heard that before.'

'I know, which is why I've been so afraid of saying it again. What I felt for you before was a schoolgirl crush, a childish fancy. I was over-whelmed by how everything had moved so quickly, by the attention of the press, and the way my parents were thrilled—the whole world was thrilled. I wanted the fairy tale, and so I bought into it.' She reached for his hand, laced her fingers through his. He didn't, at least, pull away or even resist. 'But this last week has shown me that love isn't a fairy tale, Leo. It's hard and painful and messy. It hurts. And yet it's also wonderful, because when I'm with you there's nowhere else I'd rather be.' Still no words from him, but she felt him squeeze her fingers slightly, and hope began to unfurl inside her. 'I love seeing you smile, hearing you laugh, feeling you inside me. And I love the fact that I've come to know you, that I can tell when you're amused or annoyed or angry or hurt. That I recognise the way you try to veil your expression and hide your pain. That I know when you're reading something that bores you in the newspaper but you keep reading anyway because you just *have* to finish the page.'

Leo's lips twitched in an almost-smile and Alyse laughed softly, no more than a breath of sound. 'Loving someone is knowing them,' she continued quietly. 'I didn't understand that at first. I thought it was a lightning bolt, or an undeniable rush of feeling. But it's more than that. It's *understanding* a person inside and out.

I can't pretend I understand you completely, but I think I'm beginning to. I'm starting to see how a childhood of pretending—a lifetime of pretending—has made you not just doubt other people's feelings, but your own. You told me you loved me when we were on television, and I was afraid to believe you. I think you were afraid to believe yourself. That's why you tried to deny it afterwards. It's why I didn't press the matter. All out of fear.'

He gazed down at their intertwined hands, his thumb sliding over her fingers. 'You did say love was scary,' he said in a low voice.

'Absolutely. It's terrifying. But I also think it's worth it—it's worth the risk of being hurt. Loneliness might be easier, but it's bleak too.' She squeezed his fingers, imbuing him with her strength. Her hope. 'I don't expect you to love me yet. I know we both need time to learn to trust each other. To know each other. But I'm asking you, Leo—I'm begging you, give us that chance. Don't turn away from our marriage just because you're not going to be king. I never cared about you being king. I was scared of being queen. I just want to be with you.'

'That's not why I turned away.'

She stilled, her fingers frozen in his. 'No?'

He took a deep breath. 'I turned away because I was afraid. Because I've learned it's easier to be the first one to pull away, before you're pushed.'

'And you thought I'd…I'd push you? Because you weren't king?'

'I don't know what I thought, to be honest.' He glanced up, his gaze hooded, his eyes dark with pain. 'I was acting on instinct, shutting down, closing up. It's what I've always done, and I knew I had to do it with you. You've had more power to hurt me than anyone else, Alyse. Do you know how utterly terrifying that is?'

She managed a shaky smile, felt the sting of tears behind her lids. 'Yes,' she answered. 'As a matter of fact, I do.'

'You're wrong, you know. I don't need time to learn to love you, or know you. I already do. I didn't mean to say that on television—the words just spilled out. It was as if I couldn't *keep* from saying them. I had to be honest about how I felt, not just to you, but to the whole world.'

Alyse felt her mouth curve in an understanding smile. 'And then as soon as you were, you wanted to take it all back.'

'Self-protection, just a little too late.'

'This is hard, no question.'

'As soon as you left the room I wanted to run after you. Take it all back. Beg—just like I used to beg my mother to spend time with me, to *love* me, or my brother not to leave.' He was quiet for a moment, his gaze still on their twined hands. 'He was a hero to me, you know. I adored him. He always looked out for me at school, he felt like the only person who really knew me—'

'And he left,' Alyse finished softly. 'He left you.'

'I can't really blame him. The atmosphere in the palace has always been toxic, and he had it worse than I did, buried under my parents' expectations.' Leo sighed and shook his head. 'But yes, he left, and it hurt. A lot. I told myself I'd never be like that again, needing someone so much, begging them to stay.'

Her heart ached and she blinked back tears. 'I'm sorry.'

'I don't know what kind of relationship we can have, now that he's back.'

'You'll find a way. Love endures, Leo. And you still love him.'

He nodded slowly. 'Yes, I suppose I do.'

It was, she knew, a big admission for him to make. And yet she needed more; *they* needed more. 'And what about us, Leo?' Alyse touched his cheek, forced him to meet her soft gaze. 'What kind of relationship can we have?'

His navy gaze bored into hers, searching for answers, and then his mouth softened in a slight smile. 'A good one, I hope. A marriage…a real marriage. If you'll have me.'

'You know I will.'

He turned his head so his lips brushed her fingers. 'I'm not saying I won't make mistakes. I will, I'm sure of it. This still terrifies me, now more than ever. I've never loved anyone before, not like this.'

'Me neither,' Alyse whispered.

'I don't want to hurt you,' he continued, his voice turning ragged. 'I love you, Alyse, so much, but I'm afraid—afraid that I will—'

'That's part of loving someone,' she answered, her voice clogged with tears, tears of happiness, of hope and relief and pure emotion, rather than sorrow. 'The joy and the pain. I'll take both, Leo, with you.'

Yet as his arms came around her and his lips found hers in a soft and unending promise, Alyse knew only joy. The joy, the wondrous joy, of being known and loved.

* * * * *

Mills & Boon® Large Print

April 2014

Mills & Boon® Large Print
May 2014

THE DIMITRAKOS PROPOSITION
Lynne Graham

HIS TEMPORARY MISTRESS
Cathy Williams

A MAN WITHOUT MERCY
Miranda Lee

THE FLAW IN HIS DIAMOND
Susan Stephens

FORGED IN THE DESERT HEAT
Maisey Yates

THE TYCOON'S DELICIOUS DISTRACTION
Maggie Cox

A DEAL WITH BENEFITS
Susanna Carr

MR (NOT QUITE) PERFECT
Jessica Hart

ENGLISH GIRL IN NEW YORK
Scarlet Wilson

THE GREEK'S TINY MIRACLE
Rebecca Winters

THE FINAL FALCON SAYS I DO
Lucy Gordon

0414 Rom LP